Praise for Lora Leigh's Loving Lies

5 Angels Fallen Angel Reviews Recommended Read "Lora Leigh has done it again. *Loving Lies* is a fantastic start to a new series. Ms. Leigh is an amazing author who has unlimited talent for writing scorching-hot erotic romance stories. *Loving Lies* has the Alpha males to die for and the kick-butt heroine that goes after what she wants. ...Ms. Leigh, you are an awesome writer, and this reviewer can never get enough of your books. *Loving Lies* is a romance that sizzles and makes the reader squirm for the next one. Hats off to Ms. Leigh for this fabulous read!"

~ Sonya, Fallen Angel Reviews

5 Stars! "*Loving Lies* is one scorching hot read. From beginning to end, the love scenes will have you drooling and ready to play with your own toys. One of the beautiful aspects of this novel is that the main characters are truly making love. They are not just having sex to fill the pages. Luckily for the reader, these two are adventurous in the bedroom. They never leave you wanting. Additionally, they are great characters out of the bedroom. ...Ms. Leigh is a world-class author and I always look forward to reading her work. Loving Lies did not disappoint."

~ Suni Farrar, Just Erotic Romance Reviews

A Perfect 10 "Ms. Leigh's *LOVING LIES* is the first in her newest series, Men of Summer and it's a steamy one.

A fan of Ms. Leigh's, I opened up *LOVING LIES* with great anticipation and eagerly began to read. From her in-depth characterization, to her intricately written storyline, Ms. Leigh writes a story that is simply unforgettable. For this reason I've chosen to bestow upon it **Romance Reviews Today's Perfect 10**. Surf on over to Samhain Publishing, pick up this delectable story and treat yourself today."

~ Sinclair Reid, Romance Reviews Today

4 ½ Hearts "*Loving Lies* takes the reader on an emotional roller coaster ride. ...Ms. Leigh is the Queen of Steam; she knows how to write a story that nearly sets the pages on fire. Her sex scenes are very explicit and hot. This reader recommends that you keep a large bucket with ice cubes near you when you read this book. ...There are two other characters that are screaming to have their own stories and this reviewer really hopes that Ms. Leigh gives Jazz and Zack their own stories. Thanks so much Ms. Leigh for this wonderful story, this reviewer couldn't stop reading it, because it kept this reader glued to the pages."

~ Danny, Love Romance

5 Stars! "Ms. Leigh gives new meaning to the phrase "That's what friends are for" in this instance. Three men, almost like brothers with one woman to protect. When Slade has to leave Jessie in the care of his friends with a "do not touch" banner plastered on her forehead, he's asking a lot. Jazz and Slade each watch over her in their own way. They also help this couple find themselves again after 5 years. (I certainly hope these loyal friends get their own women and stories soon!) ...Be prepared to read this in one sitting because you can't put it down once you start. Try not to slap your significant other upside the head because "he's a guy" while you're reading, too!"

~ Holly, Euro-Reviews

"A **5 Pink Hats Off Salute to Lora Leigh** for writing a story with characters so alive and filled with emotion that you can't help but be pulled into their story. Jessie's first and only love is Slade. Slade's love for Jessie is so strong he worries that she may not be able to handle it. What's a girl to do - she seduces him. What follows is a weekend of steaming hot love. ...Love will find a way...This story is very good and the reason we love to read romance novels. *Loving Lies* is one for the keeper shelf."

~ MA, The Pink Posse

"*Loving Lies* by Lora Leigh is a magnificent book. This warm hearted tale is filled with erotic passion. The raw emotions the characters express seem genuine and real. ...Ms. Leigh captures stimulating sensuality and passion in her powerful love scenes. The sexual hunger that surrounds Jessie and Slade made my heart skip a beat. The intense attraction grabs the reader at the beginning and pulls them along for an erotically sensual ride. *Loving Lies* is the first of the Men of Summer series. I am breathless with anticipation for the next heat wave to start."

~ Ophelia, Erotic Escapades

"Loving Lies has got to be one of the best contemporary books I've ever had the pleasure of reading! As is one of Lora Leigh's trademarks, every single character is well-defined and vivid enough to come to life in the mind of the reader. ...I could feel the happiness, the worry, the heartbreak, the anticipation, the joy, the love, and of course the erotic sensuality, throughout. A tale that can effect this kind of emotional intensity so deeply that it brings tears of joy and sorrow to the reader's eyes is top-notch, and you may rest assured that Loving Lies by Lora Leigh is a first-class example of that!"

~ LindseyAnn Denson, Ecataromance.com

"*Loving Lies* tore at my heart...The writing of Lora Leigh continues to amaze me. Loving Lies has to be one of the finest books she has written, and I know it is one of the most outstanding books I have read in an extremely long time. When a book makes me cry, angry, and shiver in anticipation all at the same time, then I know it is well written. Loving Lies took me full circle; from ecstasy to hate, to despair and finally love. I highly recommend Loving Lies to any reader as it is electrically charged, erotic, and just a sinfully good read!"

~ Talia Ricci, Joyfully Reviewed

Loving Lies

The Men of Summer

By Lora Leigh

A SAMHAIN PUBLISHING, LTD. publication

Samhain Publishing, Ltd.
PO Box 2206
Stow OH 44224

First Samhain Publishing, Ltd. electronic publication: February 2006
First Samhain Publishing, Ltd. print publication: June 2006

Loving Lies

The Men of Summer

By Lora Leigh

Chapter One
Loudoun, Tennessee

The music was a gentle swell of sound around the riverbank clearing. It was here the gang gathered together for a weekend of drinking, fishing and a general redneck helluva good time. It was the first gathering of the summer and it looked like the crowd was all here. Just as they had been for the last decade. The boys of summer were back again and ready to forget the cares and woes of weekday reality.

RVs, tents, pickup trucks and a various assortment of vehicles were pulled to the edge of the camping area where a bonfire burned in the center. Shouted welcomes and laughter filled the forested valley along the riverbank as music vibrated through the area with enough force to make certain no wildlife ventured near.

The flickering light cast an eerie glow about the forest behind it, even as it illuminated the revelry of those around the fire. The party was pumping, drinks were flowing and Slade Colter had a headache splitting across his forehead with enough force to give the music a run for its money. But even worse was the hard-on throbbing in his jeans. It was so engorged, so ready, so intent on one little woman that he couldn't trust himself to stay. Couldn't trust himself not to terrify her.

He should have known better than to head out here this weekend. He should have done as he first intended, what he was dead set on now. Heading to the sheltered spot further along the camping area that extended for miles along the valley of what had once been a wilderness teeming with history.

Slade hit the automatic roller to the awning and watched it fold slowly to the edge of the roof before jumping inside the vehicular home and moving into the driver's seat. With a quick flick of his wrist, he turned the motor over and began to slowly back out of the clearing. The powerful purr of the motor sent a surge of satisfaction racing through his system as he moved from the motor homes and vehicles parked around him, before turning and heading for the main road. He ignored the calls from the partygoers outside, maneuvered the awkward RV onto the road, and with a quick turn of the wheel directed it away from the party and to the private camping spot he had rented closer to town.

As the music receded behind him, he sighed in relief, watching as the headlights reflected off the road and lit the way through the darkness. Beyond, darkness beckoned, peace awaited. Or at least he hoped so. His head was so fucking messed up right now he didn't know if he would ever figure out what those words meant again.

Freedom. He knew he might as well forget what that meant. This was his last weekend in the mountains for a while, possibly a long while. He had thought that spending it with the men he had grown up with was the perfect prescription for the restlessness filling him, but it wasn't. It was making it worse. And he'd be damned if he didn't get away from the sight of laughing brown eyes and a teasing smile of one sweet little thing, Jessica "Jessie" Benton, then he was going to fuck up what chance he had of ever finding peace.

He shook his head, hoping to clear it of the alcoholic haze and the image of that innocent, tempting vision. She was so damned short she made him feel like a giant. Barely five-three, sweetly curved and celebrating her twenty-first birthday this weekend. Dressed in a bikini that had his eyes popping out of their sockets, and sporting a sexy little tattoo that kept peeking from the low band of the bottoms, demanding he get a closer look. She had his dick making a fool out of him.

He lowered his hand from the wheel and readjusted his dumb flesh beneath his jeans. He hadn't even been able to change into the swimming trunks he brought with him because of her. He couldn't get his damned hard-on to go down long enough to even contemplate it.

This was a fine fix, he told himself brutally. He had been waiting for over five years for Jessie to hit that magical age before making his move on her. He had warned off more damned pricks than he should have gotten away with, and spent too many nights jacking off thinking about her.

He pushed his fingers through his thick blond hair, a flare of sensation racing down his spine as he remembered the feel of her fingers there that first summer night.

"Slade, I don't intend to wait on you forever." Her soft laughter had sent heat curling through his gut. *"A girl can only wait so long."*

He had made some mocking comment, laughing down at her upraised face, wanting nothing more than to kiss those pale pink lips. But he had waited. Twenty-one, he reminded himself. He was a man, not a kid, and at twenty-seven he was getting closer to thirty than he even wanted to admit to. And he sure as hell wasn't innocent.

"Stupid fuck," he muttered as he turned the RV along the main road, heading for the privacy of his own camping spot. The parties were in the main clearings rather than the smaller, private areas closer to town.

He needed to escape the temptation of those velvet brown eyes. He had to think about this, he told himself. Jessie wasn't a one-night stand, and he damned well knew it. He could feel the bands wrapping around his neck, his hunger for one sweet little woman tying his gut into so many knots he had to fight to breathe. Not to mention what it was doing to his cock.

Shaking his head, Slade made the sharp turn that headed up the narrow lane toward his parking area. The RV hookups weren't as efficient there, but the peace of the dark, quiet nights made up for it. Pulling into the paved spot just large enough for the RV, he cut the motor before jumping out and connecting the water and sewer lines. Velvet darkness wrapped around him, pulled at him as a sultry breeze whipped over his naked chest.

Drawing in a deep breath, he pushed the main control of the awning, watching as it extended over him while his fingers worked at his jeans. The damned hard-on was killing him. Within seconds, his jeans were tossed carelessly to the metal rod that anchored the awning to the RV and his cock was pointing out from his body in demand.

A steady breeze whispered through the night, wrapping around him, as soft and warm as Jessie's hands.

What the hell was wrong with him? He had never had a problem going after what he wanted, and damned if he didn't want her. Hell, he needed her and he knew it. No one else had been able to still the raging hunger riding him day and night as her birthday drew closer. God knew he had tried.

He'd spent a week the month before fucking his former F.B.I. partner Amy Jennings dry, night after night, and it still hadn't helped. He thought of Jessie. He dreamed of Jessie. Why the hell didn't he just fuck her and get it over with?

Because he wouldn't just be fucking her and he knew it. Because once he had her, his footloose bachelor days were at an end and that was all there was to it.

One of his foster fathers had warned him years ago that he would find a woman who would rip his guts to pieces and make a wedding band seem like a haven rather than a yoke, and Slade hadn't believed him. He believed him now. Hell, he had believed him years ago when he found himself watching Jessie, imagining her naked beneath him, all that intensity and fire in her eyes transferred into passion.

The sounds of the night enfolded him, the call of the bullfrogs, crickets chattering in the woods around him, and catfish croaking from the bank of the narrow river that flowed in the distance. A symphony that filled his soul and partially eased the restlessness rolling through him.

It wasn't helping his hard-on.

"Do you always camp naked, Slade? This is something a girl could get used to, ya know."

He stiffened at the amusement, the breathless hunger in the voice from the doorway.

Turning, he stared at her, framed in the low light of the interior lamp, that fucking bikini baring her curves, her tanned flesh gleaming in the soft light as she tilted her head, long brown hair flowing over her shoulder.

"What the hell are you doing here?" he growled, pushing his fingers through his hair as his cock jerked at the shy little look she directed toward it.

"I was napping." A smile curved her pouty pink lips. "You told me I could use your bed anytime I needed to hide. Remember?"

Hell yes, he remembered. Last summer, when Deke Austin had been watching her with nothing but damned sex filling his mind, making her nervous as hell.

"Shit." He moved to the doorway, forcing her to back up as he stepped into the RV, facing her in the narrow confines of the small main compartment. "Dammit, Jessie, why the hell do you think I left the party?"

She moved back slowly, bumping into the small bar behind the low couch as she watched him warily, hungrily.

"I didn't know you were leaving, Slade." Her gaze flickered every few moments to his hard dick and she swallowed nervously. "I was asleep, I swear. Billy wouldn't leave me alone on the bank so Ron sent me to hide for a while until he found him a distraction. Your RV was closest and you weren't in it. I was just going to lie down for a few minutes."

She had been in his bed all this time. Stretched out on the queen-sized mattress, that golden body relaxed, waiting for him. The bedroom in the RV was the only closed-in space, and the largest.

"How long have you been awake, Jessie?" He moved to the small refrigerator, opened it and pulled a beer free. If he didn't find something else to do with his hands, then he was going to end up touching her.

She cleared her throat at his question. "Not long."

He stared at her as he popped the top of the can, his brow arching in mockery. She couldn't lie worth a damn. Never had been able to. He wasn't going to ask her how long, he knew. She would have woken up when the motor started, she would have known where he was headed.

He tipped his head back, draining half the bitter brew in a desperate attempt to keep from going to her, to hold back the lust filling him, just for a few more minutes.

"I'm sorry, Slade. I should have let you know sooner," she said as he slapped the can to the counter beside him.

His hand raked down his chest, his fingers gripping his cock for a second before a growl rumbled in his chest.

"I hope you know what the hell you were doing when you laid back in that bed and waited for me to park," he snapped, his voice harsh, the demon-lust pounding through his veins like a firestorm, searing him in his need to touch her. "Dammit to hell, Jessie. I've tried everything I know to stay the hell away from you—"

"Why?" Her breathing was faster now, those pretty breasts rising and falling, drawing his gaze like a magnet he couldn't resist. "I've been chasing you since I turned sixteen, Slade. You didn't have to stay away."

He moved past her slowly, sitting down heavily on the wide couch and staring at her as he fought the instinctive urge to jerk her to him instead. His fingers wrapped around his cock once again, stroking it idly as the blood thundered in his veins. She was watching the action, her tongue dampening her full lips with a quick little lick that had his balls drawing up to the base of his cock.

"Do you have any idea what the hell you're letting yourself in for?" He groaned. "I'm not a kid, Jessie. I'm twenty-seven years old with a hell of a lot more experience than you can imagine and needs you couldn't begin to guess."

A smile edged at her lips.

"I know you spanked Melissa Lorring," she said, the amusement doing nothing to cover her arousal. "Right before you took her butt. And I know you used Val Sheridan's toys on her. She has an extensive collection I hear. And let's see, Jazz Lancing swears you were fucking

Massey Landers in clear view at one of his parties last year, with nothing but her dress covering the act as you stood behind her." A frown veed between her brows as she stared back at him, her eyes appearing darker, her cheeks flushed. "There's not a lot you do, Slade, that I don't hear about. And Amy Jennings is crowing far and wide that you're hers forever and ever amen after the week you spent screwing her to death last month." A spark of jealous anger filled her voice. "You could have waited just a little longer, you know."

No, he couldn't have. If he hadn't spent the week fucking Amy to hell and back then he would have ended up kidnapping Jessie and scaring the shit out of her. At least, that was what he thought. Watching her now, he wasn't so certain she would have been scared.

"So you think you know what to expect, little girl?" He grunted. "You think I won't want to do every damned bit of what you just described, and more? Trust me, you haven't heard the half of it yet."

"I told you, I'm yours." She spread her arms, indicating the bikini-clad body driving him insane. "What more can I do, Slade..." She came to him then, one small step at a time. "Beg?"

Stepping between his thighs, she leaned closer. He stared into the innocent heat and arousal reflecting in her gaze and knew he was drowning. Drowning in the pure, white-hot need that exploded between them.

His hand speared through her hair, dragging her head down as he forced her lips to his. Sweet, sharp little kisses fueled his hunger. The melting of lips, the battle to

17

breathe as their heads tilted and they consumed the taste of each other.

Her busy tongue licked at his before drawing back. His lips tugged at hers, sipped from them, tasted the inexperience and the raging need, and became all the more intense for her unknowing sexuality. She was a temptress, unaware of her own power, of the violent lust she aroused within him. Struggling back from him, she stared into his eyes and smiled a mysterious, dangerous smile of feminine awareness before she dropped to her knees in front of him. Her hands gripped his spread knees as she knelt between them.

"Or maybe this." Her head lowered, taking him in a kiss that incinerated his control and any second thoughts he may have had.

"Sweet God!" His head fell back as she licked up his cock. Hot satin heat spread from the base of his dick to the thick, throbbing head as her tongue stroked him. She wiggled a bit there, probed a bit here, until his hips lifted and one hand gripped her hair as the other held his cock and aimed it for her mouth. "Open up, baby."

She opened. Slade watched, lust burning inside him as her pink lips parted, covered the bulging head and sucked him into her mouth. It was a pleasure so destructive, so all consuming he could do nothing but lose himself to it. She wiped away reality, stole his soul.

"Son of a bitch." His hand tightened in her hair as her tongue licked, her mouth sucked. She was inexperienced, but what she lacked in knowledge she more than made up for in hot, sweet pleasure. The wet, sucking sounds of her mouth over his cock were stealing his control, causing his flesh to tighten further, to spill a copious amount of pre-come into her hot mouth. She lapped it up like the little sex kitten she was, humming in approval of his taste.

"Like this, baby." Both hands moved to her hair and began to direct her. "Slow and easy, sweetheart. Suck it like your favorite lollipop. There you go..." He was panting as her tongue swirled over his tight flesh, her mouth moving up and down a second before that hot tongue probed at the head.

"Sweet baby," he whispered. His fingers tangled in the silken strands as her soft hands wrapped around the base of his erection. She began a slow, gliding, stroking action along the rest of the shaft as her hot lips destroyed him.

"So pretty..." And she was. The most beautiful creation he had ever laid eyes on. "There you go, baby, suck me slow and hot, just like that. God, your fucking tongue is killing me." She stroked, licked, sucked, taking him nearly to her throat before pulling back, only to sink down on him again. Her lips, tongue and mouth surrounded him with damp heat.

Her eyes gleamed up at him, heavy-lidded, dark with wonder as he fucked her mouth. And if she wasn't careful she was going to end this phase of the game way before he was ready for it.

"Enough." He lifted her head, tugging at her hair as a dark, deep moan left her lips.

"Like that?" He pulled at her hair again, watching as his dick slid free of her lips with a small pop.

"Don't make me stop." Her hands were busy little things, moving over the stiff flesh even as he drew her to him.

"Shh, baby. Come up here." He wrapped his hands around her curvy waist, lifting her to her feet as he rose from the couch, looming over her, his hands sliding up her narrow waist until they paused just below her heaving breasts.

"You have no fucking idea how much I want you," he growled. "You've been like a fever in my blood ever since you turned sixteen. A sweet little baby with no clue how depraved I could get with that soft body of yours."

A secretive smile tilted her lips.

"Are you going to spank me?" she whispered. She was a temptress, a soft little sex baggage and he was going to take what he had come to consider his. "Be careful, Slade, I might like it."

He knew she would. But first—first there was one need he couldn't control any longer. Her kiss. Those pouty, soft lips that wrapped around his cock had other business to attend to now. Namely, his tongue.

He lowered his head, watching her breath catch, her eyes flutter as a whimpering cry left her throat a second before he took her lips. He should have made allowances for her innocence, he knew. He should have started out soft, should have eased her into it. But God he was hungry for it. He needed to taste her worse than he needed to breathe right now.

She was sweet heat. She was a fire he couldn't extinguish inside his soul—and she was his.

His lips moved over hers, his tongue pressing past as a gasp left her lips. A heated whimper echoed from her throat and her hands lifted, sliding into his hair, gripping the thick strands as she arched against him.

Fuck yeah! She tasted like midnight. Like a hot summer night. Her tongue met his hesitantly as he swept in, a rough growl leaving his throat as his lips slanted over hers and he jerked her to him.

His hands moved up her back as he twined his tongue with hers, finding the small catch to the bikini top and jerking it loose. He could feel her trembling against him, her fingers pulling at his hair as his lips ate at hers. He couldn't get enough of her, couldn't kiss her deeply enough, strongly enough, couldn't convince himself he was tying her to him fast enough.

Within seconds he had the top released, tossing it carelessly to the side and not really caring where it fell. And then her breasts were pressing into his chest. Hot little nipples, hard as pebbles, poked into his flesh, bringing a rumbling groan to his throat as he tore his lips from hers.

"Come here." Feeling her knees grip his hips, he lifted her to his chest, turning and moving through the opened door that led into the bedroom. The bed. He had to get her to the fucking bed before he took her on the couch. And it was a possibility. Damn, he was so hot, so ready to fuck he could feel the sizzle of impending release tingling at the base of his spine.

"Slade..." Her soft, heated voice stole his sanity. "Oh God, Slade, I've waited forever for you touch me."

He had waited forever to touch her. So many years. He could feel them weighing on his shoulders, his soul. She was his. By God, she belonged to him and no one else. He'd be damned if he'd let another man have her. Never. Not as long as he lived.

Holding her in his arms was natural, right. She was a living flame warming all the cold places that existed within himself, filling the lonely corners and surrounding him with light.

As he laid her back on the wide bed, staring down at the rapid movements of her swollen breasts, her gently rounded tummy and the tattoo peeking above the band of her bikini bottoms, Slade knew he had found something he had searched for most of his life. A sense of belonging.

Long, dark strands of hair haloed her face and head, spreading out on the pillow like a fan as her dark eyes watched him with heated need. Her arms stretched above her head, arching her breasts higher, a deliberate temptation he had to grit his teeth to refuse. His cock demanded he take her and take her now, but there were so many ways he needed to touch her. Love her.

"You're beautiful," he breathed as he moved to stretch out beside her, his lips finding the fragrant hollow of her throat as her head fell back, her neck arching to his caress.

A trembling moan left her lips as she shuddered in response to his fingers moving to her tight nipples. Caressing her neck with his lips, teeth and tongue, he let his thumb and forefinger grip one hard bud, exerting just enough pressure to test her limits for the pleasure/pain he knew he could give her.

God, she was so young. Too young to know how dark, how intense sex could be. How far he could push her as he stole the illusion of control from her.

She lifted her breasts to him, a ragged cry filling the night a second before his lips took hers again, his tongue plunging deep into her mouth as he began to push her. He wanted all of her. Every shred of control, her last inhibition, the innocence that was so much a part of her and filled him with such hunger.

He filled his hands with her breasts, his fingers tormenting her nipples as she began to move beneath him. Her hands gripped his hair now, pulling at the strands to hold him closer, to take his kiss deeper as he consumed her. Hell, she was consuming him.

The sight of those bikini bottoms were still tempting him. Even now, his mind focused on her kiss, on the hard mounds beneath his hand, all he could think about was that damned tattoo. He had to see it. Breaking off the kiss, he spread hard, hungry kisses down the line of her throat as one hand moved over her trembling stomach to the material shielding the soft flesh of her pussy.

He didn't have the control to move easily, to ease her into anything. He pushed his hand beneath the material then stilled in shock at what met his touch.

"Fuck," he breathed roughly, lifting his head to stare into her dazed eyes. "What the hell have you done?"

Rising to his knees, he gripped the band circling her hips and tore the fragile material from her. Just that easy, the scraps of fabric ripped from her body and were tossed carelessly to the floor. He reached for the light overhead and flipped it on.

She lay before him, silken flesh glistening with a satin sheen, bared to his gaze, his touch. The tender folds devoid of the soft curls that should have been there. She had waxed. There was no evidence of shaving, no look of roughness or redness—the flesh was just soft, natural and glistening with a thick layer of feminine cream that had his mouth watering in hunger.

He was dying to touch. To open her with his fingers, to taste her with his tongue. The peaches-and-cream flesh gleamed in temptation as his gaze lifted to the small tattoo just above her thigh. A small smile tilted his lips.

Fanciful, like Jessie was. The dragon breathed out a flame, but had a decidedly feminine air to it. The soft colors of the dragon pulled at what little light shone from the front of RV and looked sexy as hell.

"That is such a 'Jessie' tattoo," he whispered, seeing the fierce, yet feminine core of Jessie that he loved so much in the whimsical creature.

"I thought you might like it." She breathed out, panting, her face flushed and lips swollen as she stared back at him. She made him crave her. Crave fucking her, hearing her screams echoing around him as she pleaded for everything he could give her. And he could give her so much.

"I love it," he whispered. "More than I should." His fingers feathered over it before moving to the swollen flesh below, feeling the sweet heat of her juices against his fingertips as he followed the narrow slit to the entrance of her vagina.

"Slade..." Her cry echoed around him as he rimmed the sweet opening, his fingertip caressing, testing it as he parted her. She was honey slick and hot cream. The feel of her dragged a groan from his lips as she lifted to him, her thighs parting further.

He needed to taste her. He watched as his fingers slid through the juices that eased from her pussy, his chest aching as he forced himself to breathe, fighting to drag enough air into his body. She stole his breath, his control. His heart. In that moment Slade realized Jessie had the control to break him, to complete him.

"You're too young," he whispered as he lifted his fingers from the sweet flesh he had been caressing. Bringing them to his lips, he ignored the shock that widened her lips as he licked at the sweetness, his cock jerking as the silky slide of her passion fed his lust.

Watching her closer, he moved his hand, lowering it to her lips as he smoothed a small amount of the sweetness over her bottom lip.

"Taste how sweet you are," he whispered. "The sweetest, softest little pussy in the world, and it's going to be mine. All mine. Isn't it, Jessie?"

A shudder ripped through her body as she watched him. Her wide, dark eyes burned into his soul as he saw the innocence that reflected in them. His Jessie was soft and sweet, and untried. Untrained to passion. Slade knew he should have left her alone, knew he should walk away, but once he tasted her, there was no denying her.

"Taste yourself," he urged her gently, despite the roughness of his voice. He needed to see her accepting the hungers that tore through her, needed to know she was immersing herself as deeply into the lust as he had been dragged into it.

A blush stole over her face before running along the slender column of her neck to the rapid rise and fall of her hard-tipped breasts. Then her tongue emerged, sweetly pink, and licked at the juice glistening on her lips before it curled around his finger.

He watched as she suckled delicately at his finger and his cock jerked violently, remembering the feel of that hot little mouth tugging at him. Sharp teeth scraped over the pad of his finger as her eyes, dark and filled with longing, gazed up at him.

She would destroy his soul, he thought, so very easily. Or she could remake his world and fill it with a light he had never imagined possible.

He prayed for the light.

Chapter Two

Staring up at Slade, Jessie could feel the tension tightening in her body as need began to outweigh innocence as well as feminine fear. Just being in the same vicinity as Slade could make her flesh heat, her womb shudder with need. As though her skin were suddenly too tight, her internal temperature too hot, she became combustible when he was around.

"I'm going to taste you, sweet baby," he whispered, a wicked smile curving his lips as his gray eyes swept over her parted thighs. "I'm going to eat you like candy. Think you can handle that?"

No. But her hips lifted to him anyway as a cry fell from her lips. She had no control, no desire for control. Nothing mattered but Slade's touch. The heat of his hands, his lips, oh God...his tongue.

He lay between her thighs, his hands cupping her rear to lift her closer as his tongue swiped through the narrow cleft of her pussy. The burning, agonizing pleasure tore through her, tightening her body with such intensity that she felt she would shatter.

But he didn't let her shatter. Gentle licks followed, short laps that caressed and burned, that made her jerk in his grip as she fought for more. A deeper caress, firmer, something to relieve the driving pulse of hunger beating in her clit. And he teased her. He didn't consume her, he didn't drive her over the edge, he kept her poised upon it.

He ate her just as he said he would. Like candy, one slow lick at a time. She twisted beneath him, her cries growing wilder as she fought for release, her hands tightening in his hair to press him closer to her humid flesh.

"Soft and sweet," he murmured against her clit. "Like liquid paradise, Jessie. That's what you are. The sweetest, softest pussy I ever imagined loving."

She wanted to scream at the pleasure, to revel in the male lust and hunger in his voice, but all she could do was whimper, arch and beg for more.

She writhed beneath him, his lips and tongue moved to her aching clit as his fingers returned to the fluttering opening of her vagina. Jessie held her breath, anticipating more, only to cry out in frustration as he licked slowly around her clit, his fingers rimming her opening. He was in no hurry. He was consuming her with decadent pleasure, humming against her flesh, his tongue circling her clit with impossibly light strokes of fire.

She couldn't bear it. She knew she couldn't bear it. Perspiration rolled from her skin as her head thrashed against the bed and she fought for a release that was always just a breath away.

"Slade, please..." she whimpered, desperation driving her now. "I've waited so long. Please don't tease me this way... Please..."

She could barely breathe, let alone plead. She could feel the tears gathering in her eyes as her nerve endings pulsed and electrical currents of pleasure raced over her flesh.

"I could eat you forever." The hoarse growl nearly had her coming, then his lips moved lower, his tongue flickering at the entrance to her pussy as she gasped then cried out raggedly for more. Oh God, just a little bit more and the tight knot of tension tormenting her womb would ease. Just a little bit.

The need racing through her was frightening. She couldn't control it, couldn't ease it. The tension only built, as did the pleasure and the shudders trembling through her body. And Slade was merciless. He thrust his tongue wickedly into her pussy as she arched to him, tormenting her, making her insane with the need for orgasm.

The sound of their moans was almost a physical caress. Slade's tore across her senses, the sound of a man completely immersed in the lust raging through him, from her. His tongue was a demon, licking, stroking, thrusting inside her as he consumed her, ate her with wicked sensuality. There was no relief, just the desperate, shuddering need for it as she lost herself in the white-hot heat swirling through her.

"Slade, please..." She was shaking, trembling, her voice unfamiliar to her own ears as she begged for orgasm.

This pleasure was too intense. She hadn't expected this, didn't know how to handle it. She had never known anything like this, even in her most vivid fantasies with only her fingers to bring her release. She felt as though she were burning alive, disintegrating beneath him. And in the midst of it, he added another torment. His finger slid through her juices before easing into the cleft of her rear, moving against the entrance to her anus firmly.

"Oh God. Slade. Slade, please..." There was no breath left to scream, barely enough left to live.

His lips and tongue moved against her with deliberate provocation then, rather than teasing thrusts and kisses. All the while, his finger probed and explored her rear further.

Her eyes flew open as she felt the tip of his finger pierce her ass before entering her slowly, stretching her, burning the flesh there with a pleasure she knew she couldn't survive.

"Oh God!" She prayed for release, because the pleasure was destroying her. "I can't... No more... No more, Slade..."

"Easy, baby girl. It's coming. Hang on for me." His finger retreated before easing through the soft cream flowing from her pussy. The slick juices prepared her before he slid in deeper, penetrating her rear as his thumb slid into the gripping opening of her pussy.

She was lost. Jessie felt her orgasm rip through her, shattering her. It tore through her with a strength that sent her senses spiraling in dizzying circles as she cried out his name.

"God yes, Jessie." He moved her fingers from his hair to his shoulders before rising between her thighs and moving into position. The thick crest of his cock nudged at her pussy, spreading the sensitized folds as she stared back at him in dazed pleasure.

"There, baby girl." A hard, savage grimace of pleasure twisted his expression as he began to work inside her. "Sweet baby. Let me have you now. All of you."

He moved then, strong, steady thrusts that worked inside her, stretching her with a pleasure/pain that tore through her mind and sent tension building through her body again. She needed. Oh God, yes, this was what she needed. He was filling her, pushing into her before one hard, piercing thrust sent him to the hilt inside her.

"Slade...Oh God, Slade..." She arched as he held her hips, trying to scream, to breathe, to adjust to the sudden intrusion inside her, stretching untried muscles, burning through her nerve endings and building the need to greater heights.

"You're so fucking tight, Jessie." His strangled growl had her jerking against him, driving him deeper. "So tight I could come now."

He moved against her, his cock sliding back, caressing nerve endings she never knew existed as he began to take her, possess her. He wasn't fucking her, he was claiming her. She could feel the brand inside her, the knowledge that nothing could ever be as good as Slade inside her body, thrusting, stroking, penetrating her with a heat and strength that stole the last of her reason.

"Help me," she gasped, suddenly uncertain what to do, the new sensations tearing through her, whipping her higher, hotter. "Slade, please." She was jerking in his grip, straining toward him as his cock shafted inside her, slow and easy, fast and hard, alternate strokes that had her head thrashing, her body shuddering.

"Easy, sweet baby." He reached out, his hand touching her cheek, his expression holding her spellbound as his body held her in suspended pleasure. "Look how pretty you are. So hot and tight, so damned sweet and innocent."

His fingers moved down her cheek to the mound of a breast.

"You're mine, Jessie," he growled, his hand returning to her hip as he began to move harder, faster. His voice became more gravelly than ever before. "Mine, baby. All fucking mine."

He leaned over her, his lips covering hers roughly as his arms surrounded her. His hips moved fiercely as he began to fuck her with a rhythm and strength that sent her exploding, flaming into orgasm again.

She felt everything. Sensation upon sensation. The feel of her vagina tightening around his cock, milking him with strong, even pulses as the hair on his chest rasped her breasts.

His tongue plunged into her mouth, claiming it as his erection claimed her pussy. His arms around her, powerful and strong, his hands buried in her hair, and oh God... She screamed into his kiss as she felt him coming.

He drove in deep, hard, a rasping growl echoing into the kiss as he jerked above her and his cock began to throb.

Fire filled her. Heated blasts of semen rushed inside her, throwing her high again, triggering another harder, deeper orgasm. She began to weep from the pleasure.

Her nails pierced his shoulders, her legs tightening around his hips, and Jessie lost herself in Slade. In that moment, the heart that belonged to him alone opened further, drew him in and her soul filled with the pleasure and the emotions rushing through her.

She had always known Slade would be hers. Always hers. Right here, in his bed, in his arms. This was where she was meant to be. What Jessie had been made for. For Slade.

Chapter Three

Brilliant heat surrounded Slade as he paced the outside of the RV the next morning, and raised his eyes to the roof more than once. He had sent Jessie up there beneath the summer sun, stealing her bikini and convincing her to enjoy the summer heat in the nude. The tan lines from the bathing suit were sexier than hell, but the thought of her lying, surrounded by nothing but sunlight, had driven him crazy.

To see the soft white globes of her ass flushed from the sun, the way he wanted to see them flushed from his hand, would have had him sweating if the heat of the day hadn't already accomplished that.

He rubbed his hand over his damp chest, pacing beneath the awning, denying himself the luxury of joining her. If he did, he was going to fuck her again. He was going to spread those pretty legs and watch his dick sink past those silky little pussy lips into the ultra-tight grip awaiting him.

His cock jerked in his cutoff jeans, reminding him how long it had waited to pierce that tempting little cunt. To feel the blazing heat, the soft silky juices as he listened to her screams ringing in his ears. And she was too tender to take him again so soon, he knew she was. Even after her shower, the silken folds of her pussy were swollen and flushed, attesting to his hard use of her throughout the night.

And she had been a virgin.

His gut clenched at that knowledge as he stalked back inside the RV and paced to the bedroom. There, on the tan blanket, was the proof of her innocence. The scarlet stain of her virginity was like a badge of honor, filling him with an overwhelming sense of pride. She could have had many lovers by now, hell, she dated enough. But she had saved her innocence, saved that sweet, lithe, little body just for him.

A smile shaped his lips, one he couldn't control. She was all his, by God, and she was going to stay that way. He'd kill the son of a bitch who dared to touch her now.

Bracing a hand on the doorframe, he continued to stare at that tiny scarlet stain, his chest tightening with emotion, the knowledge that his days as a bachelor were well and truly over. He was going to marry her. No way was he going to give those rednecks pricks panting after her a chance to think they could take her from him. She was his. His. The word echoed through his head as he shifted the erection beneath what had once been loose cutoffs, but were now filled with his demanding dick.

He raised his eyes to the ceiling, imagining her up there, glistening with tanning oil, stretched on the padded lounger, her silken hair fanning around her head as it had done the night before. Damn, just the thought of it was making him hot. At this rate, he was fucking going to have heatstroke.

He couldn't take her again, he reminded himself, his head dropping as a groan left his throat. He had taken her too hard the night before, there was no way that sweet little pussy was going to grip him without hurting her.

But there were other ways. The thought had his dick screaming. *Yes. Go for it. Yeah boy.* He could love her with his lips and tongue, and then fill her soft mouth with his cock and feel her sucking his balls dry. God, that would be good, beneath the blazing sun, kneeling before that chair, pushing past her lips, fucking her mouth with soft, easy strokes as her lips and tongue blew his mind and his cock.

Then he could turn her to her back, spread her thighs and have her for lunch.

His fingers were sliding the metal snaps free as he turned and headed outside, gripping the ladder that led to the roof. He couldn't wait. He had never been this horny for a woman in his life. Even the week he spent trying to fuck the image of Jessie out of his mind hadn't been this intense. This hunger was eating him alive and making him shake with the need to take her.

He moved up the ladder, his bare feet soundless on the carpeted rungs as he made his way to the sun deck. And there she was, as naked as his lust, shimmering with the thick coat of tanning oil he had applied to her silken flesh earlier before forcing himself away from her.

She lay on the open-sided lounger, her head pillowed on her arms, breathing slow and deep as the rays of the sun painted a path of warmth along her naked back, buttocks and slender legs.

Her hair was pulled into a ponytail high on her head. That would have to go. He liked her hair long and loose, liked feeling its softness against his calloused palms as he held her to him.

His cutoffs dropped to the deck as he moved toward her. He felt only one thing. Lust. Knew only one desire, to fuck them both senseless once again. She was a drug in his system, and he knew it. One there was no cure from, and he sure as hell wasn't about to attempt going cold turkey after having had her. No, Jessie was a pleasure he would never get enough of, and he intended to gorge himself on her taste and her touch, every chance he had.

Her head lifted, her brown eyes gleaming with knowledge. Her gaze lowered to his raging hard-on before lifting to his face as he dropped to his knees in front of her.

Slade didn't say a word. He couldn't speak past the baseball-sized lump that lust had left in his throat. He moved his hands to her hair, pulling the loose elastic band free and tangling his fingers in the thick mass as his dick nudged at her lips.

She licked over the head, but didn't open for the thick crest pressing against them. She smiled instead, a slow, taunting curve of her lips that had him growling like an animal in rut.

The fingers of one hand tightened in her hair as his other hand lowered, cupping her jaw and exerting just enough pressure to force her mouth open. The head of his cock slid smoothly inside and his jaw tightened with pleasure. Hot, rich, electric need raced up his spine as she sucked him to her throat. Pulling back, her fiery little tongue flickered beneath the head, laving that ultrasensitive area before her mouth sank down again. He wrapped his fingers around the shaft, holding back, forcing himself not to press deeper. Slade began to thrust past her lips, holding her head still, twisting his hips, screwing inside her mouth with desperate thrusts as the moist suckling sent his senses reeling.

Her hands gripped his thighs as she held herself steady, working her mouth over his erection like he had taught her several times the night before, yet still the touch was inexperienced enough to cause his breath to catch at her continued innocence. But what she lacked in experience, she made up for in hunger. She sucked him like a favorite treat, humming in pleasure as he began to pant in lust, watching his cock fill her mouth, feeling her tongue tease and tempt until his balls drew up tight to the base of his erection and he felt a shiver of impending release rake up his spine.

"I'm going to come." He stared into her eyes as he warned her of the explosion to come. "Hold me tight, baby, I'm going to fill that pretty mouth if you don't stop, and if I do, you'll swallow every fucking drop." The thought of her taking him so intimately, his semen pulsing over her tongue, the intimate taste filling her mouth, was overwhelming.

She hummed in response, her eyes darkening as her mouth tightened on him.

"Do you like that, sweet thing?" He groaned. "Do you like knowing you have my nuts tied in knots at the thought of fucking your mouth until I shoot every drop of seed in them down your throat?"

Her face flushed further, but her eyes glowed with arousal. That was how he wanted her, so fucking hot she would rival the sun for her heat.

"That's what you're going to get." He clenched his teeth, trying to hold back, trying to relish the sight of her sucking his rigid flesh just a few seconds longer.

His cock had other ideas. Before he could control the impulse, his balls jerked, fire raced up his spine and he was holding himself to her throat, his fingers tight in her hair. Her eyes widened, her throat working convulsively as he felt his semen rush from the tip of his cock.

"Fuck! Son of a bitch!" He threw his head back, shuddering as he filled her mouth, feeling her swallow, suck, lick, drawing every damned drop of cum from his throbbing cock until he was forced to pull back rather than begin again.

"Wait." Her voice was rough as she tried to follow him, her eyes dazed with passion. Her swollen lips pouted at his retreat.

"Hell, I can't get enough of you," he groaned, pressing her to the lounger as he moved behind her. Urging her legs apart, he jerked the bottle of oil from the side of the reclining chair. "You said you heard about me?" he growled, his hand smoothing over the sweet curves of her ass. "You heard what I like?"

She shuddered, her hips twitching, lifting to him.

"Whatever you want," she moaned, her voice husky, vibrating with arousal. "I told you that, Slade. Everything you want."

He parted the curves of her rear, staring at the little pucker hidden within it, the soft pink flesh surrounding it. It was so tiny, a tight haven for his cock, a dark, heated portal to spend the hunger consuming him.

He jerked to his feet, ignoring her whimper as he lifted her, pulled the pad from the lounger and tossed it to the deck beneath his feet.

"Lie down, baby. On your stomach." He pushed her to the cushioned pad, spreading her thighs, lifting her knees until her ass was raised before him, the entrance he sought peeking from between the gentle cheeks.

"It will hurt at first," he warned her, knowing he couldn't let the erotic pain surprise her. "You'll have to relax, sweetheart. Press out to me. You can't fight me, even for a minute."

He lifted the bottle of oil, dribbling the heated slickness along the narrow cleft as his fingers caught it and began to work it against the flexing entrance. She was whimpering, exciting growls of female demand leaving her throat as he worked the finger into her, watching the hole part for him before pulling back, adding more oil, then joining that finger with the second.

She flinched, a startled cry leaving her lips as he pressed both digits in and worked them in small screwing motions inside her. The hot cries spilling from her lips were filled with pleasure though, rather than denial. He pulled free, added more of the slick oil before beginning to work the third finger in with the first two.

She pressed back, opening for him as a startled cry left her lips and a tremor raced up her spine. But she took him, clenching around his fingers as he fucked them inside her slow and easy, scissoring them, stretching the snug muscles. His chest tightened and his breathing began to rasp from his throat.

He pulled free seconds later, coated his cock with the oil then pressed the head against the pink entrance.

"Breathe in, baby," he crooned as he parted the cheeks wide and began to stretch the little hole. "Now out, breathe out and take me, Jessie. Give me your ass, baby."

She gave. Screaming in pleasure, her pussy weeping against the fingers he placed over it to be certain it was pleasure rather than agony he was giving her. He watched his cock sink inside her, one slow, torturous inch at a time as every muscle in his body strained to hold back.

He was sweating furiously, blinking back the moisture dripping into his eyes as he watched the tiny entrance open wide for the length of steel-hard cock impaling it. Breathing hurt, because the pleasure was so fucking good. Because her cries were filled with shocked arousal and pleas for more and her pussy was drenched with the juices flowing from her.

He swore he would take her slow and easy. That he would ease her into this new experience, show her all the gentleness he could rake out of his soul. He was taking the final bit of virginity she possessed. His dick had now taken every portal possible and there wasn't a doubt in his mind she belonged to him, body and soul. He could afford to go slow. To slide his cock in as he watched her clench around it. To ease back, watching the oil-slick flesh as it stretched her, penetrated her, until he could slide in. That lasted for all of a minute before his hips jerked and he watched in amazement as his body stole control from his mind and his cock slammed inside her.

She shuddered, a strangled scream leaving her throat.

"God, yes," she cried, pushing back, impaling her ass harder on the spike-hard flesh invading it. "Harder, Slade. Oh God, yes, fuck me, fuck me harder."

He was a man possessed. Out of control. One hand gripped her hip as the other speared two fingers deep inside her pussy as he moved over her. His cock began to thrust hard and fast inside her, his hips pumping into the soft cheeks of her ass as he reamed her with delicious abandon. There were no pleas to stop, to go easy.

"Yes," her cries echoed around him. "Harder, Slade..." Her hips pumped harshly beneath him, pushing him harder up her ass as his fingers fucked her cunt. "Ah yes. It's so thick. Oh God, Slade, you're killing me... So hard... Harder...fuck my ass harder...harder..."

He growled, a demented sound of lust. He drove them both over the edge, feeling her pussy clench, convulse, erupt. The muscles of her ass clamped down on his cock, milking the seed from his balls and sending him careening into a bliss that had a strangled cry spilling from his own lips as he pumped his seed deep inside her hot little ass.

Jessie was in shock. She lay beneath Slade's body, shuddering in the aftereffects of a blinding orgasm, feeling his cock twitching. It filled her rear, spurting stream after stream of semen inside her, heating her anus with each spurt as he shuddered above her.

She couldn't believe... Pleasure and pain, in equal force, had torn through her as he impaled her ass, filling her until she was certain she couldn't take more, and yet she had, taken more, begged for more, screamed for it.

Yes, she had heard of his fascination for this particular act, how he teased and cajoled and convinced the few lovers who had allowed it. They had claimed it was highly overrated. Jessie was certain they had to have lost their minds. She wanted more, well, not right now maybe, but definitely later.

"Sweet baby," he crooned, and she trembled as his lips stroked her shoulder. He moved, pulling his still-hard cock free of the tight grip she had on it. "We're going to kill each other at this rate."

She whimpered. He popped free of her ass, feeling the heated slide of his semen as it followed his exit.

"Hmm, I'll die happy then." A tired smile curved her lips. She refused to move, small shudders still racing through her body. He smoothed a hand over her back, her buttocks, lingering to caress the heated curves gently as he collapsed beside her.

"You're going to burn if you stay up here much longer." He brushed her hair from her face as she opened her eyes, staring back at him drowsily.

He wasn't handsome, not really. Not that she had eyes for anyone else, but his sharp, arrogant features could never be described as good-looking. High cheekbones, an aristocratic nose that held a slight crook where it had been broken during a fight. A small scar slashed across the edge of his stubborn chin, another cut through the fierce dark blond brow over his left eye.

He was tall, over six-foot, and made her feel so protected, so feminine when he covered her, that the sensation caused her chest to ache. His body was lean and muscled, hard from the years of demanding physical work he performed with the construction company he had started with his two best friends. His hands were wide and long-fingered, and brought the most incredible pleasure imaginable.

"You better stop looking at me like that." A smile curved those hard, sexy lips. Not too full, but well formed and sexy as all get out.

"I can't help it." She was almost slurring her words she was so relaxed now. "You're a sex god, Slade. I think I've died and hit paradise."

He chuckled, the sound dark and never failing to cause her tummy to clench in response.

"Then you're a goddess." His hand lifted, smoothing the hair tossed over her cheek by a playful breeze, behind her ear. "Hell, if I'd had any idea what you had in store for me, I would have kidnapped you when you turned eighteen."

"You should have." She stretched as she turned to her back, her eyes closing against the rays of the sun, and tried to hide her regret from him. "I was willing."

"You're too young," he sighed, his hand moving to her stomach, his fingers sending frissons of pleasure racing through her system as he stroked the skin there. "I should be horse-whipped for fucking you the way I have. You're too tender..."

She sat up, turning to stare at him incredulously.

"You know, Slade, just because I'm not as experienced as the other women you've been screwing a path through, doesn't mean I don't know what sex is, or that I'm too damned stupid to understand the rumors of what you like. I wasn't aware there was an age limit on arousal."

He lifted a brow in surprise as his eyes roved her nakedness, darkening to a stormy gray.

"Hell, honey," he finally sighed. "Sometimes I'm not comfortable with the things I've imagined doing with you. I feel like a damned pervert already."

"Why?" She stared at him, confused. "I enjoyed it. I trust you not to hurt me, or to stop if there's something I don't like. Is there something more I'm unaware of that goes along with this?" She waved her hand to indicate their nakedness.

He propped his head on his hand as he watched her, the other reaching out to stroke idly down her arm.

"I want to tie you down to my bed, spank your ass till you orgasm from it, then shove a butt plug up it so that when I fuck that tiny little pussy of yours it will feel like you're taking a baseball bat rather than my cock. And after I've finished shooting every drop of cum torturing my balls inside you, I want to spank you again just for the sheer pleasure of watching that pretty little ass blush and that bare pussy spill its juices."

She blinked in shock, her ass clenching, her pussy fluttering in interest.

"Hell, Jessie, you're supposed to run screaming, not stare at me as though I just offered you diamonds." He groaned as he collapsed back on the deck, one powerful forearm covering his eyes. "Hell, I think you're braver than I am."

She couldn't speak. All she could think about was the image he left in her mind and the decadent arousal consuming her.

"I'm young, not a moron," she snapped, fighting to control the impulse to suggest that they do that now. Right now. She didn't want to wait, no matter how sore her body was. "What, is there some law that says I can't be interested?"

She had been a virgin, not a social misfit. She knew well what sex was, as well as the different variations on it. She had cousins. They liked to talk. And they didn't mind sharing the details with their younger kin. They believed preparation was everything.

"There should be," he grunted, lifting his arm to give her a dark, sexy look. "The things I want to do to you are probably illegal in every state of the union."

She rolled her eyes, staring back at him in challenge. "Well, I wouldn't want to break the law. I guess I'll just have to start saying no instead. I'm sure I can manage. Ask Billy and Deke, I tell them no all the time."

A frown instantly marred his brow as he rose, staring at her possessively. That look had her heart screaming in joy.

"Those two little bastards," he snarled. "They'll piss me off one time too many and I'll jerk their dicks off."

"Why?" She blinked at him in false innocence. "I'm too young for you, remember?"

He smiled, a hard curve of his lips that had nothing to do with amusement. "Baby, don't tempt the beast. I'll rip those little pricks end from end then I'll tie you to my bed and fuck you until you're too damned exhausted to blink, let alone torment me further."

She leaned forward, bracing her hands against his shoulders, her lips barely a breath from his.

"As long as I'm yours," she whispered, staring into his eyes as her own narrowed warningly. "No more Amys, Melissas or whoever else you've fucked over the past years, Slade. I don't share."

He jerked her to him, his lips covering hers, stealing her breath as his tongue plunged into her mouth, staking a claim on her kiss that he had already staked on her body.

"Neither do I, baby," he growled as he pulled back. "Remember that for good. Now get up and pull that shirt on I gave you. If I'm not mistaken, good ole Uncle Ron is riding to the rescue. I'm pretty sure that's his truck I hear heading this way."

Her eyes widened as she cursed beneath her breath. Scrambling from his arms, she searched for the shirt he had given her earlier. The sound of the pickup was drawing closer as she secured the last button on the short-sleeve, dark blue man's shirt, checking to make certain it adequately covered her. Slade drew her toward the ladder, his cutoffs once again covering his lean hips and thighs.

Tight, hard abs tempted her fingers as he passed her, but she refrained, barely, from reaching out and testing their hard-packed power once again. In response, his hand settled on her hip as they stepped back to the ground, watching as the beat-up, four-wheel drive pickup drew into the clearing with the self-proclaimed uncle to all, Ron, at the wheel, looking less than pleased.

Chapter Four

Uncle Ron, Ron Jackman, was a lean, grizzled, hard-living salesman with a pleasant smile that could turn dangerous in less time than it took a man to draw breath. The glint in his pale blue eyes was less than comforting as he stepped up to the RV and stared Slade in the eye for a long moment. When he turned to Jessie, his smile was easy, lazy, but with a hint of steel.

"Well, at least you're alive," he grunted as Slade curled his arm around her shoulders, pulling her closer to him. "Rhonda was afraid we lost you in the dark somewhere last night until Jazz finally pulled his head out of his rear and remembered you coming in here to hide from Billy."

His voice was a deep baritone, radiating friendliness despite the suspicion in his eyes as he turned back to Slade. "You could have let me know you had her. We've been searching everywhere for her."

Something Slade should have thought of. Most of the men who gathered at the parties watched out for the women who came there, especially the younger ones.

Jessie was especially looked after, considering some of the new riffraff showing up on the lake in the past few years.

"Sorry about that, Ron." Jessie leaned closer to Slade, the warmth of her seeping into his very pores as his arm tightened on her. "I should have thought to call you. I just didn't think about it."

Rhonda had been watching out for Jessie as long as she had been coming to the parties. She was one of the special girls Rhonda had taken under her wing long ago. You didn't mess with her babies and get away with it.

Ron ran his hand over his dark cheeks, his gaze slicing to Slade again. Slade hid his smile, knowing the other man was just waiting to tear into him. There could be no mistaking the fact that he and Jessie were now lovers. And Slade had no intention of trying to hide it.

"Why don't you go on in and see if I stocked the fridge with anything for lunch." He kissed the top of her head as his hand ran down her back, everything inside him rejecting the idea of letting her go.

"Why? So the two of you can argue about why I'm here?" She laughed, genuine amusement rather than anger shining in her eyes as she turned her face up to him. "You two are watching each other like a pair of dogs ready to square off. I wouldn't be here if it wasn't where I wanted to be."

Slade smiled back at her, a rakish smile that brought a flush of heat to her cheeks and hunger to her eyes.

"Go on, minx." He smacked her rear, ignoring the playful swipe she took to his head as she turned and bounced inside the RV, sliding the door closed with a smart little snap.

Slade turned back to Ron, crossing his arms over his chest, and stared at the other man silently.

Scratching his chest in irritation, Ron shook his head before a cold, thin smile shaped his lips.

"You should get rid of your garbage 'fore taking on something that sweet," he growled, nodding toward the RV where Jessie searched the kitchen.

"What the hell are you talking about?" Slade frowned, confusion knitting his brows as Ron grimaced.

"Amy's at the clearing looking for you. She's driven us crazy running that four-wheeler of her uncle's around the parked vehicles. You're damned lucky only a few of us know you like to come here. I doubt it would be pretty if she found you holed up with Jessie." His gaze was sharp, suspicious. "I hope you're not playing with that kid, Slade. I wouldn't be happy."

Ron wasn't prone to comment or concern himself with other's affairs. He kept his private business private and allowed others the same consideration. The fact that he was giving the warning was due more to the affectionate protectiveness Jessie inspired in the men who gathered together each weekend.

"What makes you happy isn't something I lay awake at night worrying about, Ron." Slade grinned to take the sting out of his words. "Come on, man, you knew this was coming the same as I did. I thought I could run from it this weekend until I turned around and realized she'd been sleeping in the RV the whole time I'd been heading out here. She's mine. I wouldn't have kept her here if I didn't intend to hold onto her."

He could feel that band tightening around his throat again. Commitment. Like an over-tight collar threatening to smother him.

Ron stared back at him, his eyes cold. It was more than evident he wasn't satisfied with the explanation.

"You better do something about the Jennings girl then. She obviously thinks she has a hold on you, and you know damned good and well she's never particularly liked Jessie."

Amy could be a mean witch at the best of times. She was a good woman, and for a while, until the past month actually, she had been his partner on a secret operation for the F.B.I in conjunction with the Office of Homeland Security. The fact that she worked for the agency and lived close enough to him that he knew her well had worked out for them and the operation. The fact that she was looking so hard for him could be a problem.

"Amy doesn't have a hold on me." Slade shook his head, trying to push away the memory that the operation they had worked on had been dropped rather than completed, and the needed information still hadn't been gained.

"You better hope she doesn't," the other man grunted, rubbing his hand roughly over his lower face. "Because if she goes after Jessie and you let her tear into her..."

"No one will hurt Jessie." The smothering sensation disappeared beneath the instinctive, furious urge to shelter Jessie.

"Make sure of it," Ron warned him firmly. "And expect Rhonda to tear you a new ass next time you see her. Jessie has been one of her babies for years, and she's worried herself to death since the girl came up missing. She won't be happy that you didn't let her know where she was."

Rhonda was Ron's wife. A petite, blonde-haired spitfire who everyone knew better than to mess with. She was friendly as hell, smiling, laughing, making everyone feel welcome. But mess with one of her babies, whether the child or person she had taken under wing was her blood or not, and she would take an iron skillet to your head. She had been known to do that on more than one occasion.

"Jazz and Zack said to tell you they're kicking your ass too." Ron smiled then. A real pleased, exuberant kind of smile that had Slade grimacing. Jazz and Zack had been his best friends all his life. They were presently partners in a rapidly growing home construction company that threatened to make them very comfortable, wealthy old men one day.

And Slade had no doubt they would kick his ass. They were usually damned good at keeping their word.

"I can see you're looking forward to it," Slade muttered. "Hell, you'd think I took off with a minor the way you're acting. She's of age, Ron."

"And I have a feeling you fucked up," Ron drawled. "And that kid you've hijacked this weekend is going to be the one to pay the price. If that happens, I'll kick your ass, and you can bet I won't leave you walking when I'm finished." His finger poked into Slade's chest, causing him to blink at Ron in shock before narrowing his eyes.

"If I fuck up and lose her, then you won't have to kick it." He knocked the other man's hand back, tensing, preparing to meet the challenge in Ron's eyes. He didn't want to tangle with the gutter fighter he knew his friend was, but he would if he had to. "If I lose her..."

He snapped his lips closed. Fuck it. "This is my business, Ron, not yours. Not now, not ever."

Ron flexed his shoulders, his anger more than apparent, even as confusing as it was. What the hell had Amy done to piss him off so hard? Slade couldn't fathom the reason behind it, but he knew he would damned sure get to the bottom of it.

"I'll take care of Amy after I take Jessie home tomorrow," he snarled, furious at the other man's interference and threats. "I'll deal with whatever the hell she thinks she's doing and Jessie won't be affected. You know better than to think I'd hurt her."

"And I don't think you'll have a choice," Ron bit out. "That's the pissy part, Slade. Amy plain pissed me off while she was out there this morning, and her smart-assed shit didn't go over real well with Rhonda either."

And when Rhonda wasn't happy, Ron got nervous.

"I'll take care of Amy." Slade pushed his fingers through his hair in irritation. What the hell could she be up to?

"Yeah, you do that," Ron muttered, jerking the door of the truck open as he glanced back at him. "And watch your ass, boy, because I think it's about to get fried."

He swung into the pickup, revved the motor, and threw his hand up in farewell as Jessie stepped from the RV. A second later he was backing away from the camp spot with a squeal of tires before he turned and headed back to the main road.

"Well, that didn't appear to be a pleasant conversation." There was a question in her voice he couldn't answer. Hell, he didn't know what was going on himself.

"You know Ron," he finally sighed. "I guess they thought the bogeyman had dragged you off last night."

"Didn't he?" She laughed up at him as he pulled her to him, her arms going around his waist. Slade pressed his face into her hair, inhaling the scent of tanning lotion, sunlight and lemon.

Amy wasn't typically a troublemaker, but she had been chasing him for months before he gave in and gave her what she seemed to want. A dumb move, he admitted. Damned dumb, and one he regretted less than a week into it. Hell, he should have just kidnapped Jessie the way he had wanted to and spent the week screwing her brains out. That would have been the smart thing to do. She would have been in his house by now, sharing his bed every night.

Which didn't seem like such a bad idea. Hell, he didn't have to run out right now and buy rings, right? She could just move in with him. He had a nice house, plenty of room for anything her little apartment held, and anything else she might want.

"So, did I bring any food?" he finally asked, pushing back his thoughts and concentrating on the sweet face staring up at him.

"If you count beer and chips as food." Her grimace assured him she didn't. "Tell you what, we could go fishing. You clean them, I'll fry them."

Surprise did nothing to still the warm surge of emotion filling him.

"Sounds good to me." He nodded abruptly. "I did think to bring bait and poles. You're in luck, sugar, the river is right real close and it's some of the best catfishing around."

*   *   *

Jessie was silent as they rested under the shade of thickly leafed trees, fishing lines thrown out into the water. She sat on one of the padded loungers he had carried from the RV for her. She watched the red and white bobber intently, not so much focused on any movement of the little ball, but focused more on Slade.

She had fantasized about him for years. Ached for him until she thought her chest would explode from the need for his touch, his kiss. He was her first lover, the only man to really touch her, to take her. And she was suddenly terrified of him.

Not physically. She had a healthy attitude toward sex, and experimenting didn't worry her in the least. Sexually, she didn't think there was anything Slade could do that would scare her away. He wasn't into sharing, and last she heard the games he liked to play weren't exactly painful.

No, it was the man she was glimpsing beyond the easy, wicked smiles and lust-filled gaze that made her suddenly self-conscious, made her aware of her own youth and inexperience.

He was twenty-seven, but he was older than her in more than just years. Four years in college, one doing only God knew what and two creating the rapidly growing construction business for which he and his friends had pooled their finances together. Rigor Construction was growing fast, its reputation and work in building homes speaking for itself. Slade had spent most of that time in Washington, D.C., working to pull in more government contracts for the building company. But there was something about Slade, about the year he spent with only infrequent visits home, that bothered her. Not that he hadn't settled in after coming back. He had, but Jessie was aware that in that year, Slade had changed in subtle, dark ways.

There was also the fact that Slade wasn't just a small-town boy anymore. He attended parties in D.C., moved in a cutthroat business world, and knew people that boggled her mind.

He looked as comfortable now, though, in cut-off jeans with bare feet, as he did in the suit he had worn when he attended a fundraiser in Washington, D.C. She doubted she could pick out a proper dress for such a party, let alone appear as confident, as self-assured as he did.

And she loved him. God, she loved him until it hurt, but the knowledge that she had no idea how to move in his world was beginning to weigh on her. She was a country girl, nothing more, nothing less. She had been raised in the mountains of Kentucky and had no desire to leave them. She wanted to settle down with the man who held her heart, have babies, do other people's taxes on the side and spend her nights in his arms.

But how could that ever be enough for him?

Amy Jennings had been quite vocal for the past weeks that she had finally snagged Slade. Despite the fact that he had spent less than a week with her, she was smug, self-assured, and confident that a ring would be forthcoming. For a while, Jessie had worried herself sick that Slade would marry the other woman. Mostly because she saw in Amy something she herself didn't possess. That same confidence and arrogance Slade wore so comfortably.

Beside her, Jessie felt like a country bumpkin in borrowed clothes.

"You're thinking too hard," Slade interrupted her thoughts, his muscled arm stretching along the back of the lounger as his hand played with the long strands of her hair.

"The fish like the quiet," she reminded him. She had no intention of sharing her fears with him. She would fake her lack of knowledge as far as she could then she would call her cousins, screaming for help. They might live states away, but they would come running if she needed them. And she had no doubt she would eventually need them.

Slade grunted at her answer. "I know you pretty well, Jess. Your eyes narrowed, and you're biting your lip. That usually means you're thinking too damned hard. It usually ends up getting someone in trouble."

She cast him a glance from the corner of her eyes. "Lucky guess," she murmured.

"Your ass," he laughed, his strong white teeth flashing in his sun-darkened face, giving him a rakish look as the thick, dark blond strands of hair fell over his brow. "Come on, baby, tell me what's wrong? Did you finally figure out what a pervert I am and change your mind about being here?" His voice was teasing, but the undercurrent of seriousness slipped through.

"I hardly think so." She rolled her eyes at the thought. If it were just the sex, she wouldn't have a problem. "Darlin', that rod you're packing is impressive as hell, but I think I can handle you."

"I think you might be right." He lowered his head, his lips pressing against her hair. "You make me hotter than hell. And you scare me to death in the same breath. It's a hell of a combination."

"I scare you?" She turned to him, folding her legs beneath her as she stared up at him in surprise. "How do I scare you?"

She couldn't imagine Slade being scared of anything or anybody.

He moved from his chair then, kneeling beside hers. He cupped her face with his large hands, their fishing rods forgotten. Gently, his thumb smoothed over her lips.

"Because you make my heart race," he whispered, his eyes stormy, his expression so serious, so intent it sent her pulse racing. "No one's ever made my heart race, Jessie. Except you. For the past three years, every time I've caught sight of you, your laughing eyes, that mysterious little smile on your face, the way you look at me in a way you don't look at anyone else. You make my dick harder than stone, but you make my heart race. You scare the hell out of me."

She felt her lips trembling. He was a hard man. He wasn't easy to get to know, or to get close to. She had known that, even years before, when she first caught sight of him while he was home from college.

"Slade, I love you." She couldn't hold the words back, couldn't have stilled them if her life had depended on it. "I know you don't love me—"

"Don't." He pressed his fingers over her lips. "Don't tell me what I feel or what I don't, Jessie. And let's not rush this. I don't want anyone else, I want to see what this is. I want to see how to make it work, okay? Just you and me, for as long as it lasts. Agreed?"

He wasn't saying the words, but what she saw in his eyes sent her heart exploding with joy. He stared at her as though she was everything. The same way her dad had always smiled at her mom, the same way she knew she watched him. It was there, and the sensations it sent spearing through her were as intense as an orgasm.

"Agreed." Her hands lifted to his wrists, her fingers flexing at the feel of his hair-roughened flesh, the warmth surrounding her. "I won't be twenty-one forever," she finally whispered, unable to still her worst fears. "I won't embarrass you—"

"Damn, woman, what the hell are you talking about?" He looked at her in surprise. "Is that why you're as nervous as a damned cat in a yard full of barking dogs? Baby girl, trust me." He lowered his head, pressing his forehead to hers as he stared into her eyes. "You could never embarrass me. Make me jealous as hell. Tie my guts into knots, but never, ever embarrass me."

His lips settled over hers, a kiss, not so much of lust, but of feeling. He moved them against hers slowly, his tongue peeking out to lick at the curves, to press into her mouth as a heartfelt moan left her lips. He wasn't taking her—he was loving her. Surely to God he was loving her. If he loved her, she could do whatever it took to fit into the world he knew. No matter what it took.

His lips whispered against hers, nibbling, licking, a slow, teasing benediction that had her breath catching in her throat. Slade raised his head and stared down at her once again, his smile gentle.

"Let's get dinner, before I snack on you again," he finally sighed. "Damn, you can make me harder faster than anything I've ever known. And there's no way you can take me again today."

She would try, if he pressed. But waiting wasn't so bad. She had waited since she was sixteen years old, she could wait a little longer.

Chapter Five

The weekend ended too soon. Jessie sat beside Slade as he pulled the RV into the parking lot at the main camp Sunday evening, dressed in another of his shirts and a pair of his sweatpants that hung on her frame despite the tie at the waist. It was that or go naked. She liked the feel of his clothes against her, his scent infusing them, reminding her of why her body was so tender and the cause of the exhaustion tugging at her.

Jazz Lancing and Zachary Richards were pulling in beside them. Slade's closest friends and his partners in the business they owned. They had gone through school and college with Slade. They were tall and tough, just as Slade was, and they were good men. Jessie had known them most of her life and she trusted them.

"Jazz and Zack." Slade's voice was filled with humor and a lazy satisfaction that filled her with pride. "I took you away and didn't let them know."

Jessie smothered her laughter. She should have told one of them where she was heading when things started getting ugly with Billy, but there hadn't been time. The regulars to the parties were very protective of the women there, though with both her and Slade missing, they should have been able to put two and two together fairly easy.

She leaned against his chest as he locked the door to the RV and held her close. The RVs parked on each side of Slade's and the motors were cut.

"Zack needs to find a woman." She grinned. "He worries too much about the rest of us. It would give him something else to do."

Slade chuckled, his cheek brushing against her hair as he bent to smooth his lips down her neck. She loved how often he touched her, always wanting her next to him, his fingers playing with her hair, his lips never far away. He didn't crowd her and many times had wanted nothing more than to just hold her. It sent a warmth flowing through her and filled all the empty places inside she had never known could exist.

"Did you drive in or do you need a ride?" His hand splayed over her stomach, his fingers rubbing against it lazily as he watched Jazz move from the driver's seat of the RV.

"A ride." She had ridden in with friends. "I could call someone." She didn't want to presume, didn't want to put him in a position that he had to offer more than he was willing to give right now.

"I have the bike. I'll take you home then run back to my place and shower and change. We could go out and eat."

"Or I could fix something?" She glanced back at him. "I'm a decent cook."

A slow smile curved his lips. "Even better. Then I could have you for dessert."

Heat exploded through her body, tightening her breasts further, sending her juices flowing from her pussy. God, she was so pathetic. All it took was a smile to send her into meltdown.

"Sounds perfect to me." It sounded more than perfect. Another night to hold him close. She could deal with that. Easily.

"Ready to roll?" He flashed her a wicked smile as Jazz and Zack were opening their doors and coming from the RVs.

"Whenever you are." She glanced back at Jazz, his arms crossed over his dark chest, a fierce frown contorting his handsome face. He didn't look pleased.

"Hey, Jazz." Slade paused, his arm dropping from her, his body tensing as the other man grunted, his dark blue eyes going over Jessie first then Slade.

"Hey, Slade," he finally drawled. "I think tomorrow I'll teach you how to use that radio you keep in that RV. You know, for little warnings when you kidnap pretty little girls."

"I kidnapped him." Jessie laughed back at the fierce visage, in no way threatened or frightened of him. "Come on, Jazz, you don't think I'm pretty enough to make a man forget to call first?"

She admitted that the knowledge Slade hadn't thought to do something that should have been second nature to him, pleased her. She had held his attention, completely.

A smile twitched Jazz's lips. "Girl, you're pretty enough to make a grown man forget his own name." His gaze flickered back to Slade, humor finally lighting the dark depths. "She's dangerous, buddy, you better watch out for her."

"I intend to do just that." Slade's arm slipped around her once again. "A very close eye."

Jessie winked at Jazz, a reminder of the warning she had given him the year before—that Slade was hers, and one day, one way, she would prove it.

The other man shook his head, his arms dropping from his chest before he wagged a finger at her.

"You're a bad girl, Jessie," he grunted. "Your daddy should have spanked you more when you were little."

"Well, if he gets lucky, maybe I'll let Slade take care of that minor bit of discipline." She held back her smile as Jazz's eyes dilated with surprise a second before he chuckled.

"I don't doubt he won't either." He turned to Slade. "Make sure you at least show up at the office on time tomorrow. We have to get that estimate together and get it out before noon."

"I'll be there." Slade urged Jesse forward. "See you tomorrow, Jazz."

The walk along the parking lot was made in silence, a relaxed, easy silence as the early evening warmth surrounded her, and Slade's hand at her back did little to calm her. The way his fingers stroked and probed, she could feel the sensations clear to her pussy. She was aroused, aching and growing hotter by the minute.

Thankfully, her apartment wasn't far from the RV lot because the hard throb of Slade's Harley beneath her wasn't helping things as she rode behind him. Her knees clasped his thighs, his back raked against her breasts, sensitizing already overly aroused nipples.

"Here you go." He pulled into the parking lot, helping her from the bike before easing off himself. "Do you have a spare key?"

She moved quickly to her car, reaching beneath the wheel mount where she kept the spare key, and headed to the door. Moments later, the door was unlocked and the security system deactivated.

"Safe and sound—" Her words were cut off as the door slammed closed. She found herself lifted, pressed against it as Slade's lips ravaged hers.

Her arms went around his neck, her fingers sinking into the wealth of dark blond hair as a whimpering sound of hunger left her throat. His tongue pressed against hers, twined with it, as his lips slanted against hers and ate at her like candy.

His hands weren't still. His hard body held her close to the door and his fingers curled around her thighs, lifting them to encase his body. He pressed the jeans-covered length of his cock into the notch of her thighs.

"I can't get enough of you," he growled, breaking the kiss, staring at her with eyes dark with lust. His fingers moved deeper between her legs, brushing against the aching entrance to her cunt as the wet heat dampened the material of the sweats she wore.

"That's a good thing." Her head fell back against the door as his lips moved to her neck, his tongue licking, his teeth raking the tender flesh.

"Not when I'm hard as hell and you need to rest." He groaned, pulling back then licking at her lips again, teasing her with his tongue the barest second. "I'm outta here, baby, before I end up fucking you against the door and ruining dessert."

He released her slowly and opened the door, before pulling her back and placing another hard kiss on her lips.

"I'll be back in a few hours. Be ready for me. We might just hit dessert before dinner."

His broad chest moved roughly as he breathed in, a grimace twisting his lips before he kissed her again, his tongue delving deep for long moments. Jessie felt her mind disintegrating beneath the dominant possessiveness of his tongue.

When he pulled back, he unwrapped her arms from his neck, brushing her lips with his thumb again. "You look pretty like that. Your lips swollen from my kiss, your eyes almost black because you want me almost as damned bad as I know I want you. Keep that look, baby, and I won't make it five minutes before I fuck you again."

"That's supposed to scare me?" She arched a brow suggestively. "You could always shower here, bad boy."

She watched the muscle jump in his jaw as he stepped back, shaking his head.

"I'll need clothes. If I'm late to the office tomorrow, Jazz and Zack both will kick my ass. Close that damned door and get in there and hide. Because when I come back, you've had it."

"I'll love it." She laughed as he groaned, pressing her back before gripping the door and closing it firmly.

Turning, Jessie leaned against it, closing her eyes, her smile still in place. Finally, Slade was hers. She would learn whatever she had to learn, and in time, she was confident she would easily meet whatever needs he had. But he held her, when she knew he wasn't one to hold his women, at least not in public. He kept her at his side, possessive, dominant. He had taken every opportunity to touch and hold her, finding a pleasure in doing so that she could see in his eyes.

Giddy pleasure filled her as a silly smile shaped her lips. Her fingers bunched in the shirt she wore. The damned thing nearly fell to her knees, but it smelled like Slade, it wrapped around her and reminded her of his touch. Warmed her.

And he was coming back, for dessert. Heat raced through her body, singed every nerve ending and had the blood pulsing fast and hot through her veins as she rushed for the shower. He was coming back and she intended to be ready for him.

Chapter Six

Amy was waiting for him when he pulled into the driveway of his home, and she wasn't alone. Sitting on the porch with her was Don Farrell, his handler at the Office of Homeland Security. Slade could feel his stomach sink as he walked slowly up to the porch, the keys to the front door in hand, some internal sense warning him that his life was about to go to hell.

"I heard you were cutting up a fuss at the campsite," he told Amy as he stepped onto the porch.

Amy wasn't really the "cutting up a fuss" sort, and as he stared at her he knew whatever reason she had made such a public showing to collect him, it had nothing to do with hurting Jess, and everything to do with destroying his life.

"She had to follow the relationship the two of you set up last year, Slade," Don explained as Slade opened the front door then stood aside so they could enter.

"That's over," he informed both of them. "So why try to continue playing the game?"

The interior of the house was cool, dim, the peace it had once held shattered as Amy and Don entered and the door closed behind them.

"Wrong. Kingston and Baines tracked us back here, Slade. The operation is back on. They made contact the other day and they're interested in the deal we were setting up for the arms. We're back on, lover." She laughed at him, as Slade felt something wither inside his chest.

Kingston and Baines were as elusive as shadows. The arms dealers were supplying weapons and ammunition to the Middle East, and the C.I.A. as well as Homeland Security were desperate to stop them. If they didn't stop them, the bloodshed was only going to get worse.

"We have a watcher who drove in last night." Amy pulled a file from her bag as she moved into the kitchen.

Slade went for the whisky. He didn't bother with a glass, he uncapped the bottle and took a hard, nerve-strengthening swig that nearly stole his breath.

"Are you okay?" Amy asked as he lowered the bottle, fighting for life rather than just breath.

"I'm listening." And dying inside.

"We had announced the engagement before the operation broke off, and Kingston and Baines are offering to host the wedding." Her smile was triumphant as she opened the file to a color picture. "This is our watcher, he arrived in town last night, and he was at the party you attended in the clearing. We'll be heading back to Washington in three weeks, compliments of Kingston and

Baines, once everything is in place. They'll hold the wedding and we'll be in."

Kingston and Baines were family men, as odd as that was. Working within the organization had taken over a year, only to have it fall through when the two brothers-in-law had pulled back from their very lucrative side business for some reason.

"Why now?" Just when he thought he had his life on track. When he thought he could finally follow his own dreams.

"Who knows? That's what we need you to find out," Don stated, his plump face sober and intense. "Find out what they're up to and get the proof on them. Let's do this while we have the chance."

"Projected length of assignment?" It wouldn't be overnight, that was for damned sure.

"Three years. From experience we know they won't move fast. They're just dipping their feet back into the arms sales right now. Your cover as suppliers will aid us in finding out exactly where those arms are going and who their contacts are. We want to round up the whole network, Slade, not just a few of them."

Three years.

He stared at Amy. The engagement they had set up before the operation had fallen through had made sense at the time. Now, it was ripping through him with razor-sharp regret.

Jessie. God, what was he going to do about Jessie? He tilted the bottle back, ignoring Amy and Don's confused looks as they watched him. He didn't owe them any fucking explanations, all he owed them was the completion of the contract he had signed. A contract that signed his soul to the Homeland Security office until this operation was finished. A completion that had been a done deal until now.

He nodded shortly. "Give me the details."

He couldn't not finish it. If Kingston and Baines ever learned he wasn't who and what he pretended to be, a construction company owner with the means and connections to procure the weapons they needed, then they would strike. They would strike first at the people closest to him. At Jessie. Jessie couldn't be hurt. He had to protect her, the only way he knew how.

*   *   *

Summer nights had always been Slade's favorite time. The breeze rushing through his hair was scented with freshly cut grass, burning charcoal and life. Peace had always enveloped him when he rode the bike on nights like this, but tonight, there was no peace.

Regret ripped through his guts with enough force to knot the muscles there, to cause his teeth to clench until they ached from the pressure. The wind whipped through his hair, the familiar scents of the mountains wrapped around him, but all he smelled was Jessie's sweet scent, and a bitter fury that could be aimed at no one but himself.

All he could think about was touching her, feeling the heated warmth of her flesh against him, the fist-tight grip of her pussy milking his cock with destructive results, hurling him into a release he couldn't refuse, no matter how much he wanted it to last. The way her eyes stared up at him, no matter what he did to her, or encouraged her to do to him, she watched him with heat and hunger.

God, what a fool he had been. Wrapping himself around her, letting that something he couldn't name fill him, only to have it ripped from him with a force that still left him gasping, fighting to breathe past the denials racing through his head. He should have just stayed home. It was senseless to do this, but he couldn't seem to let it go. He had to see her, one last time, convince himself more than her that the past weekend had been a mistake they were both going to have to put behind them.

He owed her that much. He couldn't leave her hoping, wondering. If he did, he would never be able to protect her in the only way he knew how. And he had to protect Jessie. Above all things, even before his own comfort, his own agonizing regret, he had to protect her.

And it was destroying him to make this ride, to follow through with what he knew he had to do. As he drove through the night, images of the weekend played before his mind. Jessie on her knees, her lips wrapped around his cock as he taught her how to pleasure him. On her back, her thighs spread, her screams filling his mind as he pushed his tongue slow and easy inside her climaxing pussy, feeling the waves of release on the fingers he had buried in her ass.

Jessie swimming naked in the water, wrapped in moonlight, daring him to join her. Or sitting against his chest as the dawn rose over the mountains, his arms wrapped around her as the fog enclosed them.

It had been a dream. A fantasy come to life, and now it was over. It was just over.

He turned the motorcycle into the small apartment complex she lived in. The neat little rows of buildings with their cheerful flowers growing along the stoops and fresh cut grass, cut into his chest. He didn't want to see cheerful when the regret was nearly eating him alive. It was just regret. It wasn't truly grief. His soul wasn't being ripped in two. He hadn't loved her, he assured himself. He cared for her. He didn't want to hurt her—hell, he had spent years protecting her until she was old enough for him. She was a beautiful woman. A sexy, hungry little kitten and he was a possessive man. That was all it had been. He didn't love her.

He parked in front of her apartment, breathing in roughly as he forced himself to move. He made his fingers uncurl, one by one, from the handgrips, before swinging from the seat. He felt like an old man, every bone and muscle protesting the journey he was about to make.

He walked up the cement walk, staring straight ahead. He had never shirked his responsibilities in his life and he wasn't going to start now. His knuckles landed heavy on the door as he felt the muscle in his cheek jumping violently in response to her call to enter.

Her voice was like honey, hot and sweet, making his dick jerk and throb with a hunger he knew had no choice but to go unquenched.

He opened the door, stepping in slowly, his gaze instantly finding her by the small dining-room table, a halo of candlelight surrounding her from the tapers she had set in the center of it.

He stopped, ensnared by her, entranced by the vision standing before him. Slender feet were encased in black heels that lifted and arched her graceful feet so erotically he almost howled in pain. A short, clinging black dress covered her breasts, cupping them, shaping the sweet mounds before sliding down her body like a fall of night.

She was so fucking beautiful that for one moment, for one blinding, weakening second he nearly took what his cock was screaming was his before doing what he knew he had to do.

Protect Jessie. The impulse was so ingrained, so profound, even the ravening hunger building inside him couldn't overrule it.

"Slade?" She tilted her head, her hair falling over her shoulder like a silken shadow as she stared back at him. "Are you okay?"

Okay? God no, he wasn't okay. He was dying inside. He stood staring at a vision any man would kill to have and he was going to turn his back on her, rip her tender heart out of her chest and walk away. He was just going to walk away, and die a thousand deaths when he did so.

He reached to his side and flipped on the overhead light, watching her blink at the sudden brightness as a glimmer of foreboding filled her gaze. The smile that had curved her lips eased away and within seconds her expression was somber.

He cleared his throat, glancing away from her, fighting for the strength, the self-control to do what he knew he was there for.

Her lips tightened, pursing as they trembled lightly, before she stilled them, her breathing beginning to accelerate. He could see the slowly dawning awareness in her eyes, the flash of horror, of denial, the pain that for a moment twisted her features and left her swaying before she gripped the back of the chair, holding tight, and facing him anyway.

God, she was so young, so beautiful, and so fucking strong that in that moment, he knew exactly what he was walking away from, and what he was headed toward. And it was going to be hell. And he had brought it all on himself.

"Just say it." He watched her steel herself. Saw the tightening of her shoulders, the knowledge that filled her eyes. Her voice was low, lacking the bitter anger he had expected, the tears he had been certain she would shed. The thought of those tears terrified him. How was he supposed to fight her tears?

"Do I have to?" he asked, not certain if he could say the words, thanking God with every thought that she knew what he had come here for, that he wouldn't have to say the words, wouldn't have to let her see it was killing him to do this.

"Oh, I've heard about that part of your relationships as well." Her voice was bleak, her words echoing with a pain she couldn't hide. "I guess I was foolish enough to think it would last longer than a weekend. I have to say, at least I broke a record. Your shortest relationship. Lucky me."

She was breaking him. She was breaking his will, ripping something inside him that he didn't know existed, with her pain-laden voice and her dark, agonized gaze.

He wanted to comfort her. Everything inside him was screaming at him to go to her, to hold her, to tell her, to explain everything. She would understand. God help him, if he had ever believed anyone had loved him in his life, he knew Jessie did and he was a goddamned fool to walk away. But he knew there was no other choice. The best gift he could give her was the lack of hope. To be a bastard in the purest sense and allow her to get on with finding someone...

He couldn't finish the thought. Sons of bitches, he would kill the prick brave enough to lay the first finger on her where he could see it. He wouldn't be able to survive if he saw another man touching her.

"I'll leave then." He had to force the words past his throat. "You were good, Jessie. Damned good. But you were right, not mature enough..." The words stuck in his throat as he watched her flinch. As though someone had laid a lash to her soul, she jerked so hard he felt the pain himself.

"I understand." She turned away from him, a shudder racing up her back as she bared the delicate naked flesh that ran to her hips. There was no back to the dress, just slender straps holding it in place.

His hands fisted. He couldn't touch her. He wouldn't touch her. But son of a bitch if it didn't hurt to breathe, to drag each lungful of air into his chest, to survive without touching her. How the hell had he let this happen? How could one person have so much power to hurt another?

And he didn't love her. It became a mantra within his mind as he watched her. But she believed she loved him, how much worse was it for her? The ragged wound digging into his very spirit became deeper at the thought.

The candles extinguished but she didn't turn around.

"Leave. Now." Her voice was low, nearly incoherent as her shoulders shuddered. "Just leave, Slade."

He pressed his lips tightly together, stilling the violence inside him, the need so overwhelming it locked in his soul and screamed out in bitterness to tell her the truth. He breathed out wearily instead, turned and did as she asked.

He left.

As the door closed behind him, Jessie felt herself collapsing, felt her breathing falter as the pain erupted in her chest. She didn't bother to find the chair or to stop the slow slide to the floor. She was only thankful the leg of the table was there to brace her back, to hold her upright as she stared before her, dazed, disbelieving.

How could she have been so wrong? It didn't make sense, he was supposed to shower and come back with a change of clothes. They were going to eat dinner, then have dessert in her bed. They were going to... Nothing.

She felt the breath hitch in her throat, felt the tears that scalded her cheeks a second before a sob echoed in lonely misery around her. For five years she had waited on him, certain more awaited her than a single fool's weekend. Certain that even if the relationship didn't work out, she would at least have the chance to try. He was a hard man, his life had been hard, but she never believed he would take her to his bed, that he would tease and promise to wait for her, if he hadn't wanted more than a weekend.

She leaned her head against the leg of the table and she cried. She had no intention of holding it back, or "bucking up" as her father called it when one of his children cried. He had never been able to handle the tears. But he wasn't here now. He was gone, and the misery inside her soul was ripping her apart. It was cry or die, and she would be damned if she would die for Slade.

She loved him. It wasn't a death sentence, she was young, and she would get over it. Right?

"Oh God." She wrapped her arms around her stomach, leaning forward with the convulsive shudder of agony that shook her from her soul outward as she heard the motorcycle start up, heard it scream from the parking lot. "I love you, Slade," she whispered, knowing that all the love in the world could never hold what wasn't hers. "I love you." And it didn't matter, not really, because she wasn't mature enough, wasn't slick enough to fit in his world. The only difference was he had realized it before it was too late, where she had continued to hope. And to dream.

Chapter Seven

The world didn't end with a broken heart. There were still classes to attend, a job to hold down, and Jessie did both on autopilot. The only difference was that she immersed herself now in both school and her job, working herself to exhaustion, praying that the night would come when she would fall asleep and she wouldn't dream of Slade.

She stayed away from the parties and the forested clearing where they were held, avoiding it with a desperation that clawed at her as each weekend rolled around. Was Slade there? Of course he was, he was a steady there, rain or shine, and there was no way she could face him, no way she could face the pity if anyone ever learned how easily, how casually he had dropped her. How deeply he had hurt her.

Even now, three weeks later, the open wound that had once been her heart, ached continually. She dreamed of him, of loving him, of hearing him whisper his love for her, of his arms surrounding her, protecting her. She awoke to a cold, lonely bed and the tears. There were enough tears to drown her.

She pulled into the parking lot of her apartment complex. She breathed out tiredly as she glimpsed the two Harleys parked beside her spot and the men resting casually on them. Jazz and Zack were good friends but it was after midnight, the shift she had pulled at the local Wal-Mart had been a hard one. She wasn't in the mood for chitchat.

She had a feeling though they were after more than chitchat.

She pulled the car into its slot, staring at the two men through the window as she shut the engine off, grabbed her purse and opened the door. They straightened from their bikes, lean, muscular bodies and eagle-eyed expressions tense and waiting.

"Hey, Jazz. Zack." She threw the strap of her purse over her shoulder as she locked her car and headed for her apartment. "What are you two up to this late?"

She pasted a cheerful smile on her face as she pushed the key into her door and glanced back at them. She restrained her sigh as she saw they had all intention of going in with her.

"Checking on you, little girl," Jazz grunted as they followed her into the apartment, closing the door and waiting as she disengaged the alarm.

"Checking up on me?" She threw her purse to the chair beside her before striding into the small kitchen. "Want a beer?"

"Yes to both questions," Zack answered as they stood in the middle of her living-room floor, waiting.

Hell, she just didn't need this. Not right now. Not until she managed to patch the open wounds inside her.

She carried three long-necks into the living room, passing each of them a cold bottle before moving past them and settling back in the large, comfortable chair that sat several feet from the front door.

The room wasn't large. It held a comfortable couch, chair, coffee table and the entertainment center that housed her small TV. But the rent was cheap and the location close to school and work.

Jazz pulled a chair from the small dining-room table, setting it across from her as he straddled it and stared at her with midnight-blue eyes. Zack sat back on the couch, one foot propped on his knee as they both watched her silently.

She hated it when these two went silent and just watched. It usually meant they were seeing much more than anyone wanted them to know.

"I'm not ready." She knew what they were after, there was no sense in playing games, but she had learned she wasn't nearly as adept at reading men as she once thought she was. "Just go away for now."

She lifted the beer, taking a long, slow drink, needing the false courage she gained from it.

Jazz glanced at his partner before staring back at her. Neither said anything as her stomach began to cramp with tension and her throat thickened with tears that were only shed in the darkness of night when she awakened in her cold, lonely bed.

"Get your bathing suit." Zack's voice brooked no refusal. "You don't have school tomorrow and you're off for the weekend—"

"Wrong." She flashed him an enraged look. She would not be forced into something she couldn't face. "I signed up for weekend classes and I had my work schedule changed—"

"And I called your fucking boss an hour ago, right after you got off work. Get changed, dammit, you're coming to the clearing if I have to carry you there."

"Why?" She slammed the bottle to the table, furious. "And who gave you leave to fuck with my schedule or my life, Zack? You're not my father or my fucking husband, so get off."

He rose to his feet.

"I don't have a problem carrying you in, girl." He smirked. "You're not going to hide like this. Everyone will figure out why—hell, they're already wondering. You're getting your butt out there and you're going to party and laugh. You and Slade both missing on the weekends is causing tongues to wag."

Her breath stopped at his name. She forced herself to breathe again, to work past the agony clenching her heart.

"What does he have to do with anything?"

"Don't play games with me, Jessie," he snarled. "He's a big boy, he wants to fuck his life up, I'm all for it. But I'll be damned if you're going to let wagging tongues hurt you. Now get that goddamned suit and let's go."

"I don't have one."

"Sure you do." Zack picked up the small bag he had carried in with him. "Here it is. We don't want excuses, you're tougher than this, Jessie—"

"Don't tell me to buck up," she snapped, pushing her fingers through her hair as she paced across the room, unable to stare them in the eye, to see the knowledge there. "I can't do it. I'm not ready."

"I don't give a damn what you think you're ready for," Jazz growled. "Get dressed and let's go."

She shook her head, tears filling her eyes. "I can't face him."

"If he's there, you won't have a choice," he snarled. "He hasn't been in three weeks, and talk is starting. I won't have you on the tip of wagging tongues, Jessie. Not like this."

She wrapped her arms around her chest, swallowing convulsively.

"It will kill me to see him..."

"It will hurt. It will rip your heart apart, but you'll smile and laugh and pretend he doesn't exist, or so help me I'm going to end up beating the hell out of him for it. So it's your choice, play the game or he'll go home from the office Monday bruised and bleeding from one end to the other."

She swung around in shock.

"Why?" she questioned, furious, hurting. They were Slade's friends. It didn't make sense that they would turn on him over her.

"Because he knew better." Jazz finished his beer, taking the bag from Zack before handing it to her. "You didn't. Now get it on and pull on some jeans and a shirt. You'll ride in with one of us, and one of us will take you home. But you are going. And you will have a good time if it kills you."

*   *   *

And it was going to kill her. The next night, exhausted, with too many beers speeding through her system, Jessie laughed and joked and partied the night away, feeling the sting of Slade's eyes on her, the pain lancing inside her.

He had pulled in hours before, securing his RV to its spot against the riverbank beside Jazz's. The bonfire was glowing on the bank, music pulsed and pounded in the air as laughter and drunken revelry filled the clearing. There had to be nearly forty people spread out along the wide clearing that led to the bank of the river.

Fourth of July weekend, she had forgotten it was even a holiday weekend. She stood beneath the awning of Ron's RV, sipping at another beer, watching the antics of the men and women shedding the week's tension and enjoying the night to its fullest. Jessie just wanted to go home. She could feel Slade watching her, no matter where she moved, his brooding gaze biting through her control as she danced too much and fought to stay one step ahead of the groping hands.

"Hey, pretty girl, when do you intend to dance with me?" Raw-boned, broad as a Mack truck and as dark as Slade was blond, Jazz moved up to the sheltered RV, watching her with quiet blue eyes despite his smile and booming voice.

His gaze flickered up the line of RVs and vehicles, stopping at Slade's before his gaze came back to her.

Jessie leaned against the side of the RV, smiling back at him as she shook her head in exasperation. "Who's going to hold the other up?" She laughed as he weaved a little drunkenly. She knew she would be no steadier on her feet than he was on his. But he had kept his promise, he hadn't hit Slade, he hadn't even acted as though he were pissed at the other man.

"We can prop each other up." He spread his arms wide. "Come on, one dance then I can find my bed and sleep like the angel I am."

She snorted at that, though she stepped carefully from beneath the dubious protection of her shelter. She was trembling at the thought of dancing, of having another man touch her, hold her. The music was slow and dreamy now, romantic, enfolding the night with a hint of passion and seductiveness.

As his arms went around her waist, she shuddered.

"Hold on, sweetie," he growled in her ear. "If you don't dance, everyone will know you're hurting. Me, Zack and Capt'n Ron are the only ones in the know right now, let's keep it that way."

He wasn't nearly as drunk as he pretended to be.

Jessie lowered her head, letting him lead her as they swayed to the music, swallowing the unbearable need for another man's arms.

"He'll drink his limit and run and hide soon," he soothed her as she shuddered again. "Just dance here with me a bit, then I'll take you to my little home away from home and let you hide there for the night. I think you've been brave enough, little soldier."

Gentleness filled his rough voice as her breath hitched and she cushioned her forehead against his shoulder.

"Tell me how to make it stop, Jazz," she whispered, weak, fighting every instinct inside her that screamed out to her to go to him, to scream in rage that he had thrown her away so carelessly.

"Takes time." He laid his head against the top of hers. "Just close your eyes, pretend he's holding you—I won't care a bit—and save face. Then you can go lick your wounds so you'll be able to do it again tomorrow. You're doing great. No one knows you're breaking inside."

His voice was at her ear, a soothing baritone that eased the shudders racing over her.

"Why does he keep watching me?" She could feel him, even now. "He won't stop."

"Because he's a dumb bastard." His hands were petting up and down her back. It would appear a caress, when it was actually a soothing gesture to ease the pain inside her.

Jazz, like Zack, was one of the good guys. Hard-working, without the dark, rough edges Slade possessed.

"We're almost done," he breathed against her ear. "One more little song and we can stumble to the RV and pretend to expend our passion. Damn, you know, if I hadn't seen you in diapers way back when, I might have been able to take advantage of it."

She laughed. Yes, he had seen her in diapers. Once. The fool.

"You're crazy, Jazz." She settled against his chest. It wasn't Slade, but Jazz only wanted a dance, not her soul.

"Yeah, I'm just a grinnin' fool," he assured her as the song ended. "Here we go now."

He pulled back from her, his arm looping over her shoulder as he led her to his RV. If she didn't know him better, she would have never stepped foot on the pervert wagon, as it had been nicknamed.

She kept her head down, grateful for the escape as they entered the darkened interior.

"Go on back, I'll sit right here and watch the damned fools out there. Someone is going to catch the hills on fire before it's over with." He pointed to the back of the RV and the bed there. "You go sleep, sweet pea. I'll stand guard."

She was too tired, too drunk and too confused to argue. She moved through the camper, entered the narrow door and crawled into the large bed there. The night was hot, but she pulled the light quilt over her, her body chilled as she fought the shudders racing through her.

"I love you, Slade," she whispered, as she had every night for the past three weeks. "Goodnight." He wasn't with her, but the words allowed her to close her eyes and let the alcohol take over as she drifted into sleep.

Chapter Eight

Jazz sat on the couch several hours later, the television turned down low as he watched some action/adventure flick he couldn't even name. His mind wasn't on the television though, it was on the woman sleeping restlessly in his bed and the man moving closer to the door of the RV.

There was no mistaking the broad form as he paused at the door, then opened it soundlessly.

"She's asleep. Leave her the hell alone."

Jazz, more than anyone, was well aware of what was going on and why Slade had walked away from the sweetest little girl Jazz had ever known. Slade could hide the truth from most people, but as a business partner, as a friend, as a foster brother, he had told Jazz the truth. And it sucked, it really did. Sometimes life just kicked your ass to hell and back and didn't even give a man a break.

"I hoped she was." Slade breathed out roughly. "I need to see her, Jazz. Just for a minute. I won't wake her."

That boy needed more than just to see Jessie and Jazz knew it. His voice echoed with lonely rage, with a hunger that wasn't about to let go of his guts. Jazz breathed in deeply. He had known it was coming, this was why he had brought Jessie to his rig rather than letting Zack take over. He was the only one who knew the truth, the only one who would allow Slade within speaking distance of her. Not that he had tried. Slade had been real careful to stay close to his own RV, drink his own beer, and just watch. Until now.

"This ain't gonna help you, Slade," he sighed, feeling the man's pain. Hell, they had all lost enough in their lives that their adult years should have flowed like candy rather than stinking like shit. "It will only make it worse."

"I'm leaving in a week." Slade kept his voice low. "I can't leave without seeing her, and this is the kindest way to do it."

Jazz glanced toward the back of the RV. It would take more than hungry eyes to awaken the exhausted girl. She would never know Slade had been there. But Jazz knew his friend was only torturing himself worse.

"Don't make me beg, Jazz," Slade said, his head raised proudly, his shoulders straight, tense. "You know the truth, just give me this and I'll never bother her again."

Jazz snorted at the statement. Some people just confounded him, as though they hadn't learned the circles of life. What he saw between these two would never just go away. And fate had a way of making folks face even their worst pains, their greatest mistakes.

"Hurry the hell up." He rose from his seat. "And I'm going with you. You touch her wrong and I'll break your arms."

Slade didn't argue. He followed Jazz, entering the small room as the other man wedged himself into a corner, crossed his arms over his chest and watched Slade's strength crumble.

It was humbling, seeing a man as strong as he knew Slade was, falter in the face of something as weak and helpless as one little girl.

Jessie had rolled to her back, the quilt still clutched in her hands, but her stomach and hips uncovered. Slade knelt beside the low bed, his fingers trembling as he touched the small dragon tattoo revealed by the dip of her bikini bottom. Just like Jessie. A fantasy, a fiery vision that could never truly be his.

He leaned forward then placed a reverent kiss on the small mark before rising and staring into her face. His fingers brushed back her hair, shook as they smoothed over her lips. He touched her like a man touches life—one terrified, light-as-air brush at a time.

He should have looked away. Jazz knew the kindest thing he could do for both of them was to give Slade a few private moments. There were some things a man just couldn't say when others were near, and Slade looked like a man who needed to clear his soul real bad. But Jazz also knew his friend's self-control wasn't at its peak. He wasn't going to let him hurt Jessie any more than he already had, even for friendship. Sometimes a man had to set friendship aside, and for Jazz, this was one of those times.

"Isn't she beautiful, Jazz?" Slade whispered, his voice almost too quiet to hear as he asked the question. "The prettiest thing in the world, I think."

Yeah, she was. But Slade didn't need that answer.

"She's like a fire in the winter. She warms you even when you don't know you're cold." Slade's voice was rough. "Take care of her for me, will you, Jazz? Don't let those bastards out there touch her. They touch her and I'll have to kill them. I won't be able to help it."

His voice was ragged, bringing a prickle of warmth to Jazz's eyes. Damn, that boy was killing himself. Jazz felt his heart clench at the emotion that filled Slade's voice, that radiated from him as he bent to the girl.

"I'll keep her safe for you, man." It was the least he could do. Slade had pulled his ass out of the fire plenty of times when they were young. "They won't touch her."

How he was going to manage that one he didn't know. But he would. Not just for Slade, but for Jessie. Sometimes you could just look at two people and see that the world had things in store for them, together. Slade and Jessie were two of those people. This wasn't over, not by a long shot. It was just being delayed a bit, for whatever reason.

He watched then as Slade bent closer, brushed a kiss over the soft lips, then laid his head next to the girl's as he whispered in her ear. What he was saying, Jazz couldn't hear, but he could hear the need, the hunger clawing through the low tone.

"I love you, Slade." The words were sleep-slurred as Jessie shifted, curling closer to Slade, her hands reaching for him before falling helplessly to the bed with a little whimper when Slade jerked back.

He was white as a sheet, his gray eyes nearly black, his hands trembling as he pushed them through his hair before curling them into fists. He stared down at Jessie, his throat working convulsively, his agonized expression lit by the glow of the moon pouring into the cabin.

"Don't let her get hurt." His voice was strangled as he turned and left the room and seconds later the RV.

Jazz glanced at the bed again, and his heart broke. Still sleeping, but tears whispered down her cheeks and when she spoke, the words were so filled with love, with need, that Jazz was forced to wipe his own eyes.

"I'm cold, Slade..."

Chapter Nine
Five years later

"Jazz, you're a slob." Jessie made her way through his RV, picking up discarded beer cans, bags of stale chips, a pair of forgotten swim shorts, still damp, that were thankfully lying on the linoleum of the small kitchen floor rather than the carpeting in the tiny living room. The man was as hopeless as falling in love. He needed a keeper, not a lover or a wife. He needed a full-time nanny.

"Yeah, so my foster mothers always said." He scratched at his lean abs, leering at her as she bent to check the oven to make certain nothing was growing there before opening the door to fully inspect it. "You could take me in hand, Jessie. I'm sure you could beat me into submission."

She looked at him from the corner of her eyes before rolling them and shaking her head.

"I wouldn't take you on a bet," she snorted as she closed the oven door. "When did I clean this place last? I could have sworn I was just in here last month working my butt off for three days straight. I have better things to do with my time, Jazz."

"Like what?" He braced his hand on the overhead ceiling beam that separated the kitchen from the living room. "Hiding in your damned apartment and nursing your broken heart? Come on, Jessie, it's been five years."

She faced him then, a frown drawing her brows together as she watched him in confusion. What the hell was up with this?

"I haven't nursed a broken heart in years," she assured him with a wave of her hand. "The apartment is quiet, and I have work to do. Keeping up with Rigor's books is a full-time job with all the projects you have going, and I have lesson plans to consider. When the summer is over I do have to go back to work. Remember?"

He grunted, his expression becoming somber, his blue eyes moody. That wasn't a good thing. When Jazz got like this, he was usually up to something. Hoping to avoid another of his "face the past" lectures, she moved through the RV, tossing the dirty clothes into the small basket that sat off the bedroom before moving back to the kitchen.

"Still telling him goodnight?"

She froze at the question. Turning slowly, she faced her dearest friend with a spark of anger.

"What the hell are you talking about?"

"I've slept with you, Jessie," he growled. "Do you think you can hide the fact that you whisper goodnight to him before you go to sleep? I have damned good hearing, baby."

She licked her lips, not out of nervousness or embarrassment, more because she just didn't want to answer the question.

"I won't discuss this with you." She moved away from him, turned on the faucet before squirting a small amount of dish soap among the dirty dishes she had placed in the sink.

"Sweet pea, if you can pretend it's him fucking you while I'm the one doing the pumping and grinding, then you can discuss this."

He ducked, just barely, as the glass flew from her hand, aiming for his head. The smile that curved his lips was pure male satisfaction.

"Fuck this," she snapped. "Clean your own damned pigsty, I'm not doing it."

She dried her hands on a nearby dishtowel, hiding the nerves that shook her fingers, the tight band that wrapped around her chest. The guilt was bad enough without him throwing it at her. Some days, it was all she could do to face him knowing what she had done. She was damned lucky it hadn't destroyed their friendship. It still might.

"Darlin', I told you I didn't mind." He blocked her as she tried to leave the RV, a gentle smile on his lips, in his eyes. "I'm simply trying to make a point here. You're not letting the past go..."

"I don't need to hear any more of your damned lectures. Between you, Zack and Ron, I've just about had enough of it." She punched her finger at his hard chest, aware that the fierce action had very little effect on him.

"Just because I'm not out spreading my legs for any damned moron with a hard cock doesn't mean I've not faced the past. Hell." She threw her hands up in exasperation. "What is there to face, Jazz? He came, he left. End of story. Goodbye, Slade. Fuck him."

"You want to fuck him so bad that just talking about him makes you wet." He wasn't angry, he wasn't fighting her. He was amused. Not laughing at her, but deliberately pushing her for whatever reason.

Jessie stepped back, propping her hands on her hips as she watched him with narrowed eyes.

"What the hell is your problem? Fine, you fucked me, I cried for him. Not just once, not just twice. So fucking what? You knew what the hell you were doing when it happened."

"Maybe I want you to fuck me for a change." He shrugged casually, and she might, *might* have believed that was all there was to it—if it wasn't for the fact that she could see the evasiveness in his eyes, the amusement lurking even deeper.

Jessie stepped back, wariness filling her now. This was a part of Jazz she didn't know how to handle. The manipulator. And damned if you could figure out what the hell he was up to until the game was up.

"What does that mean?" She shook her head warily.

"Exactly what I said." He dropped his arms, his lips curving up in a smile that most women swooned for. "Maybe the next time I'm petting you all over and holding you against me, I want you to think of me, instead of Slade Colter."

Jessie turned away from him, pushing her fingers through her hair before wrapping her arms across her chest. She hadn't really slept with Jazz often. Just enough to get through a few bad nights, not enough to risk either of their hearts. Usually whenever he was between women, and when she needed more than a cold bed and a dream to ease the restlessness that clawed at her chest. But not enough to ease the pain. She had cried each time, curling away from him, hating herself for her weakness.

She was over Slade now though. She hadn't awakened crying out for him in nearly two years. Sometimes, sometimes his name was on the tip of her tongue, but she had loved him for so many years that she felt it only natural.

"I don't think of Slade." She wasn't going to fight him, but even as she said the words she knew she was lying. She hung her head, staring at the floor as she clenched her teeth against the fury the thought brought.

"You still whisper goodnight to him, even if you're asleep when you do it, Jess," he finally sighed. "You still whisper his name when you get cold, and go all quiet and moody if we talk about him. You don't date—"

"I date all the time," she retorted without heat.

"Wimpy little boys who don't have a chance of measuring up against Slade. I bet their dicks are tiny and their brains even smaller. Forget that." He snapped his fingers, raising his eyes as though in prayer before gazing at her again. "You don't actually fuck them, how would you know?"

"I fucked you," she snarled. "See, letting the past go."

"You fuck me because you think I'm safe," he grunted. "Well, maybe I want more now."

That shocked her. She stared back at him, aware that her surprise was showing as her hands bunched in the cover-up she wore over her bathing suit.

"Want more?" She frowned, shaking her head.

"Yeah. More." He nodded slowly. "Maybe I want you to fall in love with me like that. I'm getting older, hell, it's time to settle down. Maybe I want to marry you."

Maybe? Maybe? What the hell was up with the maybes? Jazz was not a "maybe" man. He always knew exactly what he wanted and went right after it. No regrets, no recriminations and philosophizing. That was his motto. Or it had been.

"And maybe you've lost your damned mind." She narrowed her eyes on him, trying to figure out what his problem could be. "You don't just decide to get married, Jazz. Doesn't work out that way."

"Maybe I'm in love with you and just don't want to risk rejection. You know what rejection does to me. Just the thought of it makes my poor little body quake in fear."

Jessie stared at him in disbelief. Turning back to the sink she began to sniff the beer cans. Someone had given him mind rot rather than rotgut.

"Funny Miss Smartypants." He laughed at her then reached out for her as she evaded his grip and headed for the exit.

"Clean this pervert wagon up," she snapped. "I'm not cleaning it again. And I'll be damned if I'll put up with your insanity either. Figure out what kind of bee is up your butt and get rid of it before I get rid of it for you."

He followed her outside quickly.

"Maybe the problem is that I want up your butt," he griped as they stepped beneath the awning. "Come on, Jess. I promise not to hurt you. Let me have your butt..."

She turned to slap at him, but a surprised cry left her as an enraged snarl sounded behind her. A second later Jazz was flying into the clearing, head first, and a tall, too-familiar figure was jumping after him.

"You lying fucker." A fist slammed into Jazz's face, throwing him backwards before he even had the chance to gain his feet. "Son of a bitch, I'll kill you."

"Ron!" Jessie screamed for the patriarch of the camp, knowing if anyone could calm the enraged beast hell-bent on breaking Jazz's head, it was Ron. He might need reinforcements. The only problem was, they weren't doing anything to help.

Fists were flying and if Jessie wasn't mistaken, there was a damned good chance someone was going to end up dead. Or hospitalized.

"Would you stop them?" She ran to Zack, gripping his powerful forearm and staring up at him pleadingly.

"Hell no. Best fun I've seen here in years," he drawled, lifting the beer in his other hand as he glanced at Ron. "My money is on Slade. He just came back and that boy has a load of pent-up pissed. Fifty bucks."

"Naw, Jazz will take him. He has staying power..." Money was being passed to Ron.

"Like hell!" Jessie snarled, fury whipping through her. She ducked the hand he reached out to attempt to catch her as she turned and raced to the two combatants.

"Enough." She pushed herself between them the moment she saw an opening, slamming both hands into Slade's hard chest as his fist came flying toward her face.

He stopped. Barely.

Jessie stared at the fist in shock. Broad, hard as a rock, scraped and bleeding and no more than an inch from her nose. Swallowing tightly she raised her eyes to his face and felt that first shocking awareness again like a punch to her womb.

Enraged gray eyes stared back at her, then at his fist, as Jazz staggered to his feet, gripping her shoulders and panting above her.

"Hell, baby, I think Slade is mad. What do you think? Was it the butt comment?"

Slade growled a curse so explicit Jessie shuddered in fear at the rage in his voice.

"Both of you are asses." She was fighting to breathe, struggling with rage, confusion, and an echo of past pain, staring at an older, harder Slade, her hands curling against his chest as the heat and sensations of pleasure began to rush through her system.

She jerked back, her teeth snapping together in self-disgust as she stared into his dark, forbidding expression. Saw the black fury that overwhelmed him as he glanced at Jazz's hands on her shoulders, looked in her eyes, then back to the hands.

She wasn't about to move. She couldn't move. She was mesmerized by him, by the savagery in his expression, the white-hot fury that turned his gray eyes black.

Slade was home. She couldn't see anything, couldn't feel anything past the fact that he was back.

"Hey, baby, I want to point out you're staring at him like he's fresh meat and you're starving. Not good for that claim of being over him, you know," Jazz spoke at her ear, his voice amused, his hands frankly caressing on her shoulders as Slade's gaze snapped to them, jerking Jessie back to reality.

"Have you lost your mind?" she sneered, pushing Jazz back as she retreated as well. He was following her lead much too easily. "Are both of you insane?"

Her face flushed with embarrassment as she caught sight of the crowd gathered behind Slade, watching in interest at the scandal unfolding before them.

"Get your fucking hands off her!" Slade's voice was low, a rough, furious growl that sent alarm shaking through Jessie.

Evidently, Jazz wasn't in his normally intelligent frame of mind.

"Hey, you gave her to me to take care of. I just did what you asked. I'm taking care of her."

Shock rocked through her system. She stared back at Slade, rage slowly burning inside her as the truth began to fill her.

"You touched her."

Jazz sighed. "Yeah. I did. And boy did I—"

Jessie slammed her elbow into his abdomen, smiling with sharp pleasure at his indrawn breath. She could feel her body shuddering from the inside out, anger eating away at her control before she stepped away from both of them.

"Gave me to him?" Her lips were shaking, her hands clenching into fists to keep the rage from exploding through her. "You dared to care one way or the fucking other what happened to me?" She was screaming, only barely aware of the tone of her voice as her arm swung, involuntarily, the anger surging so hard and fast inside her that she wasn't aware of what she was doing until she felt the shock of her fist connecting with his jaw.

His head jerked to the side then swung back, his gaze piercing, his body tight, his expression drawn into lines of dangerous, soul-deep rage.

"Before you hit me, I do need to point out that I've been a very good boy lately." Jazz held his hands in front of him, smiling despite the bloodied, bruised condition of his face. "I even promise to clean my pervert wagon."

He wasn't in the least regretful. He didn't show even an ounce of remorse. Jessie could feel the eyes on her, dozens watching the scene in fascination. She stepped back from both men, tears filling her eyes as betrayal washed through her.

"You have no right." She pointed a shaky finger toward Slade. "No right. You know it and I know it."

He didn't speak. He stared back at her, the storm raging in his eyes, his expression stoic as he watched her.

"You are mine!" The snarling claim left her blinking in shock.

"Yours?" She drew herself carefully erect, a mocking smile twisting her lips as she felt the pain, the humiliation she had felt for years wrap around her. "No, Slade. I haven't been yours for a very, very long time. And I never will be again." She turned, sneering at the three men who had refused to help her earlier. "There's a bet for you, boys. But if I were you, I'd put my money on me."

She turned, stomping away from them, uncaring if they killed each other. She pushed through the crowd, moving to the RV she now wished she had burned as she had once considered. It was the location of her greatest pain. By God, she could still burn it.

"Now look what you did," Jazz snapped as they both watched Jessie's RV peel from the line of vehicles and begin down the lane toward the main road. "She's leaving, and she's going to pout on me for weeks. You sure as hell know how to crash a party, Slade."

Slade couldn't take his eyes off Jessie. Her shoulders were stiff and straight within the dimly lit interior of the RV driver's seat. Staring straight head, she didn't look toward him, she didn't look back. This wasn't the woman he had left. The one who never yelled, who always laughed, whose eyes sparkled with light and love.

This was the woman he had left in her apartment, crumpled on the floor, dejection marring every line of her body. He had seen her through the partially opened slats of the shades that night, watched her melt to the floor, saw the tears that coursed down her face as she stared straight ahead. There had been no sobs, no screams, just a silent misery he had never forgotten. A misery that matched the one that built inside him with each year away from her.

As the crowd moved away, he was left staring at Jazz, Zack and Ron. The three men held varying degrees of suspicion and sympathy. Finally Zack shook his head.

"You should have called, Slade. I could have warned you."

He hadn't called anyone other than Jazz. Only Jazz had seen the pain and rage killing him, only Jazz had allowed him what he needed to walk away from Jessie. He turned back to his friend, his eyes narrowed, rage eating away at him.

"Hit me again, and I'll hit back," Jazz murmured, the words reaching his ears only. "We can talk or we can fight. Your choice."

They were brothers in a sense. Slade, Jazz and Zack had come together in the boys' home outside town more than two decades ago. All unwanted, considered too wild, too uncontrollable for adoption. They were fostered out often, but they always returned. And they stuck together.

Slade would have never imagined Jazz would betray him so thoroughly as to take Jessie to his bed. To touch her, God, love her. Had she forgotten him that easily? Hell no, she hadn't. She couldn't have, because his soul had died without her, only breathing, only living again with his return.

"Get fucked," Slade snapped, pushing past the other man and heading for his cycle. He knew where she was going, it was as instinctive to her as it had been to him. He knew it. Felt it in his soul. She would go to the little camping spot where he had parked his RV once before, the one place where the silence and the peace of the land could soothe whatever pain filled them.

"Oh, no you don't, buddy." Jazz swung him around, jumping back before Slade could strike out. "You're not going after her. You left her, remember? Five years, man. She's not yours anymore."

The hell she wasn't.

"Are you claiming her?" Slade hated to kill a friend, but he'd be damned if he'd let anyone else stand between him and Jessie.

"Don't push me, Slade. Jessie will decide what she wants, not me, not you. Now let's go talk, or we can fight. Those are your only choices. Going after her right now is not an option."

Slade clenched his fists, determined to knock Jazz out of the way and head out for the woman who had tormented him for five long, agonizing years. Before he could, Jazz, Zack and Ron moved around him.

"Might as well have a drink and forget it, son." Ron pushed a beer into his hand, his smile cold. Hard. "You're not going anywhere tonight."

"Come on, Slade." Zack slapped him on the shoulder, his unsmiling face lacking hostility, but filled with determination. "You'd do the same thing. Let her get used to the idea that you're back, no matter how big an ass you made of yourself. We all need to talk anyway, it's been a long time, and there's a hell of a lot you didn't tell us before you left." There was recrimination in his voice.

His gaze sliced back to Jazz.

The grinning fool shrugged. "Hey, they saw you leaving my RV that last night, and their fists are almost as hard as yours. I like to stay pretty, you know." He worked his jaw with one hand. "Let's go share a stiff drink, man. Your fists have gotten stronger."

Slade wanted to shake his head, to force himself back to reality. His best friend had slept with the woman who held Slade's soul and he was supposed to share a drink with him?

"She was dying inside, man," Jazz told him softly. "She whispered your name, she cried for you, and I let her pretend. Which was better? Me or one of those yahoos?" He waved his hand toward the crowd behind them, his words reaching no further than Slade's ears. "I saved her for you, man, just like I promised." A wicked smile crossed his face. "Maybe. I'm thinking though...maybe I could win her from you."

Jazz sauntered off as Slade stared at his back broodingly. What the hell was up with the maybes?

Chapter Ten

She owned the RV Slade had sold, so there really wasn't any place to run that Slade couldn't find her. But she had no intention of running. She didn't head to the small campsite, suspecting he would follow her. She drove back to her apartment instead, climbing the steps outside the offices of Rigor Construction to the large apartment she had rented from Jazz and Zack several years before. She locked the door carefully, set the security then moved through the darkened living room to her bedroom.

It had been Slade's apartment as well. He had slept here, in that big bed, sometimes for weeks on end while he was building his house. He had just finished the house the month before that ill-fated weekend they had spent together. Until then, this had been his home.

No, she had never gotten over him, she thought as she moved into the bedroom. She had never forgotten, something inside her had refused to let her release the past.

She had installed sliding doors on the back wall of the bedroom, complete with a locking screen door to allow the fresh summer breeze into the room while securing her safety on summer nights. Outside, the balcony Jazz and Zack built beckoned her, if only the weariness tearing through her would subside. She opened the glass doors, leaving the screen secured before stripping and crawling into the bed, staring through the screen into the darkened night as she let herself get used to the fact that Slade was back. Harder, broader. A more dangerous Slade. One she was no more immune to now than she had been five years before.

She wiped her hands over her face, breathing out roughly as she fought to make sense of his return. He had left her five years before. After an incredible weekend of sex, he had walked away, claiming her immaturity as the reason he didn't want her, and three weeks later had disappeared, taking Amy Jennings with him. Experienced, sophisticated Amy Jennings had married him, lived with him.

The news that Amy had died several months before in D.C. had reached the gossips in town a few days ago, but Jessie hadn't expected Slade to return. Why would he? There was nothing left here for him.

She grimaced at the pain that surged through her. The knowledge that another woman had claimed him had nearly destroyed her when she found out. That had been the first night she had slept with Jazz. Crying out Slade's name, holding onto another man as he whispered the right words and let her pretend, if only for a little while, that she hadn't been a fool, that she hadn't lost the only person she knew she would ever truly love.

She remembered her shame when she awoke the next morning. How she cringed away from him, her stomach clenching as bile rose to her throat.

It's okay, sweet pea. It's just me and you. Friends. Use me, Jessie, there's no shame in it when no lies are whispered. You don't love me. I don't love you. Let me make this easier.

She had been so weak. Too weak. Over the years she and Jazz had fallen into a rut of sorts. When the loneliness was too much to bear, he was there. And he never cared that it was Slade she craved. That even in her sleep, she still called out to him.

She consoled herself that it had been over a year since she had lain with Jazz. That in the five years since Slade left, she could count less than a dozen times that she allowed Jazz into her bed. A dozen times too many, she readily admitted.

"Fool!" she snarled to herself, her fist beating on the bed as she gritted her teeth against the anger surging through her.

And why should she be angry? Why should she feel shame? Slade left her.

She bounded from the bed, pacing through the apartment as she let the anger rise. Better the anger than the arousal. She refused to feel arousal. Her fingers curled as she remembered the heat and hardness of his chest beneath her palms, remembered the way he stared at her, eating her with his eyes even as they swirled with rage. But even worse, she remembered her response to it. Lightning hot, surging through her bloodstream, awakening a hunger inside her she hadn't known since he had last touched her.

And she hated it.

A strangled scream of fury left her throat.

"You son of a bitch," she snarled. "Bastard. Unconscionable, whoreson, asshole..."

"Your language has definitely gone downhill. Jazz hasn't been a good influence on you."

She jerked around, staring at the opened balcony screen, her heart racing. Slade stood there, large as life, leaning against the doorframe as he watched her.

"Did you kill him?" If he didn't, she would.

A mocking snort left his lips. "He's not worth killing. I think you might have weakened his mind though. All those damned maybes were getting on my nerves."

"Why are you here?" She suddenly felt less than comfortable as she jerked her robe from a chair and tied it firmly.

He stepped into the room, closing the door behind him, his expression shadowed, his eyes pinpoints of hungry lust. She could feel it in the air around her, swirling, shimmering between them. Her breasts tightened as she watched him, her nipples pressing against the robe. The waxed folds of her pussy began to dampen with a layer of her juices.

He glanced at the bed.

"Do you want to take this to the living room, Jessie? Or do we do it here?"

She swallowed tightly.

"I can tell you what a bastard you are just as easy here as I can anywhere else, Slade." She smiled with sharp mockery, pretending her body wasn't screaming out for his touch.

"If you can do it while my dick is slamming into that tight little pussy, you go for it." He shrugged as though it didn't matter. "But it will be. And you will be screaming. It's up to you."

She felt a sizzling heat race over her scalp before spreading through her body. It struck her clit like a whip of lightning, sending a pulse of hard, aching need that almost took her breath.

"So confident," she crooned mockingly, allowing her lips to lift in a sneer as she raked her gaze over him. She would not notice how damned good he looked. Snug jeans cupping an obvious arousal, a dark T-shirt stretched over his broad, muscular chest. His face was leaner, harder, his gaze not just hungry, but bordering on ravenous.

"Confident?" he mused, his brow arching as his gaze went over her again. "If that's how you want to see it. It doesn't really matter at this point. It's going to happen. Does it happen now or do we talk first?"

"It doesn't happen at all," she snarled. "You left, Slade. Remember? I wasn't mature enough for you." The wound that was her heart bled at the memory. "Do you remember any of that, Slade?" she threw back at him furiously, five years of pain and rage erupting inside her. "Do you remember how you did it? Do you remember how easily you did it? Guess what, stud, I didn't think much of the 'dessert' you provided."

His expression contorted for a second, a pain-filled grimace that smoothed out as quickly as it came.

Breathing roughly, she whirled away from him, trembling as she fought to hold back the surge of violence raging through her. She stalked through the living room and into the kitchen, fighting the shaking of her limbs, the hunger that seared her with impotent fury.

"I was wrong."

For the second time that night she threw a glass. It shattered against the wall over his head as he ducked, moving quickly to the side while shards rained around him.

"It's too late," she screamed, fists clenched at her side, five years of agony tearing through her as the cause of the loneliness, the aching cold that filled her, and the pain, stood before her unscathed.

"I won't accept that." His voice was low, too controlled, too patient as he moved toward her.

"You don't have a choice." Bitter laughter escaped her throat as she refused to retreat, standing before him, watching him, hating the arousal slicing through her, the pain tearing at her. "Are you going to rape me, Slade? Will you take something that hasn't been yours for five years now?"

"I'll make it up to you, Jessie." His voice throbbed with dark need.

"Will you, Slade?" She stared up at him, the fury and violence that ate at her tearing her apart. "Can you go back in time? Can you take away what you did? Can you make me fucking forget you married another woman and left with her no more than weeks after fucking my heart into the ground?"

"Jessie..."

"Guess what, stud?" Her laughter ripped from her chest. "I don't even fucking care now. You don't fucking matter. I haven't missed you in—"

Before she could evade him, he jerked her to him, his head lowering, his lips stilling the rage spewing from her even as it ignited five years of desperate need. His tongue plunged into her mouth as he dragged her into his chest, his head tilting, lips slanting over hers, eating at her lips. A hoarse moan ripped from her throat at the pleasure exploding through her. Her hands flew to his shoulders, nails biting deep as his hunger, his lust, began to fuel hers.

His lips nipped at hers to force them open, his tongue plunging inside again as one hand threaded through her hair, gripped the thick strands and pulled her head back sharply.

Deeper, remorseless, the ravishment of her mouth swept through her senses as they both seemed to feed to the other the lost dreams, the hunger, the aching emptiness of the years past. A burning brand of heat raced through her as she fought to get closer, battled to purge the bond that held her within the grip of one weekend's worth of memories. One man's touch. This man's hunger.

"Did Jazz please you, baby girl?" He tore his lips from hers, his voice graveled, assured. "Did you come with him until you begged him to make it stop? Did he make you hotter every time he touched you?"

The fingers in her hair held her head in place as his lips drew back from his teeth, the primal snarl on his face almost terrifying to behold.

"No..." she snapped back, hating the satisfaction that filled him. "He did it right the first time."

He threw her away from him, barely catching her as she stumbled over a kitchen chair, righting her before he stalked to the other side of the room, his breathing harsh, fury radiating from the tenseness of his body as he kept his back to her.

"You're going to cause me to kill a man," he snarled. "One I grew up with, trusted with my life." He swung back to her, spearing her with the livid depths of his eyes. "Don't do that, baby..."

"Don't call me that," she bit out, her voice rough. "I'm not your baby, I'm not your anything. Not yours and not Jazz's. The two of you can fuck each other for all I care."

"I like your ass better," he growled. "Now is the wrong time to lie to me, Jessie. Hate me if you have to, curse me if you need to, but don't fucking lie to me about this."

"You have no right to demand anything," she yelled back, her heart pounding, her pussy weeping. She hated him. Hated everything he had done to her, made her feel, everything she couldn't forget. She hated him. Just as fiercely as she hungered for him.

"Get out." She was crying. She could feel the tears washing down her cheeks now, and had another reason to hate. "You didn't want me then, and I don't want you now."

"Liar." There was no heat in his voice, no anger. "I hurt you. God knows I've paid for it a million times over in the last five years. I lied to you and I left you. And I have no right to be here. I know all that, Jessie. But it won't change the fact that I am back, and I won't let you go. Not now. Not ever again."

"And nothing will change the fact that I don't want you here. Clean the wax out of your ears, hillbilly. Fuck off."

His lips quirked in amusement. "I missed you, Jessie."

"I never thought of you once." She waved her hand dismissively, fighting the weakness filling her, the need to touch him, to be touched by him.

"Not even once?" He sighed, looking around the apartment. "That explains why you bought my camper. Why you sleep in my bed, here. Why not so much as a thread of the carpet has changed in five years. Do you dream of me, Jessie? Like I dreamed of you? Hot, deep, filling every particle of your soul until you awake drenched in sweat, aching for release?"

"And you had release, didn't you, Slade?" She couldn't forget that. Could never forget it. "Amy was there—"

"Amy is something we have to talk about," he gritted out, a grimace twisting his face. "God knows we have to. I need to explain—"

"Why should you?" The shudders were ripping through her body. She didn't want to hear explanations.

She didn't want to know what made Amy the better woman. She knew the other woman had walked away with the man who held her soul. What else mattered? "Why the fuck should you care, Slade? I wasn't mature enough—"

"Don't." He shook his head, staring back at her fiercely before raking his fingers over his shortened hair. He hunched his shoulders in weariness.

"Don't what? Remind you of what you said? What you did?" She shook her head, exhausted. "You're right, what's the point? It didn't matter to you then, and it doesn't matter to me now."

She turned, walking away from him, fighting years of wasted dreams and a need she couldn't destroy. She was worse than a junkie. There had been nights, just as he said, she awoke sweating, crying, reaching for him. Needing her fix.

"Take Jazz to your bed again and I'll kill him," he said as he moved to the front door, his eyes blazing at her in the dim light of the living room. "Don't test me on this, Jessie."

"Maybe I love Jazz now, Slade," she shot back. "Five years is a long time. Maybe it's time to let the past go."

He turned, a slow lethal move that had her tensing warily.

"Don't start with the damned maybes, I've had enough from that grinning loon out at the lake. And stay away from him, Jessie. I'll kill him. I'll kill any man who touches you now. Remember that."

The door jerked open, only to slam behind him a second later, leaving her to stare at his back incredulously. She had no doubt he meant every word of it.

Chapter Eleven

Slade didn't leave. He moved into the apartment next to her, sliding open the bedroom window, knowing any sound that came from the opposite room next to his own balcony would be clearly heard. He couldn't leave her. He couldn't walk away.

He sat in the chair beside his own sliding door, staring at his hands as he listened to her rage, listened to her cry. She ripped his heart out a thousand times over with her vows that she didn't fucking care, then gave him hope each time he heard the aching hunger in her voice when she cried his name.

The offices of Rigor Construction were set outside town, the large building holding three apartments, one downstairs and two upstairs. Zack, like Slade, had built his own home even further from town, leaving the upstairs rooms free. There were no neighbors here, no reason for anyone to stand near, to hear Jessie's agonized voice screaming out at him. He couldn't have stood that. Couldn't have stood for anyone else to hear her pain, to know his own.

He had left her five years before, the threat of the danger he could bring to her too overwhelming. And the operation had been left uncompleted. It was his responsibility. He had signed on. And God only knew the regret that had eaten him alive for five long years.

The wedding had gotten him in place with Kingston and Baines, then Amy had taken it a step further. She had gotten pregnant. One of the few nights he had shared her bed, and she had been waiting on him. The child had been no more to her than a ticket to push Slade deeper into the organization they were mired within. But the proof had come in. He had collected the evidence, had worked steadily to take down the men he called friends, and to keep a handle on a wife determined to get them all killed.

He had believed Cody was his child, that he knew Amy well enough to be able to trust her. He hadn't realized how deeply involved she had become with the organization, or how it would threaten his life, and the child he claimed as his own.

God, how he had craved Jessie over the years. He had hungered with a desperation that never stilled, that only grew. He poured over the emails that bastard Jazz sent, often. Pictures. He had never imagined the other man was sleeping with her, that he was taking what Slade believed belonged to him alone.

He wiped his hands over his face as dawn peeked over the horizon, realizing that Jessie's sobs had stilled and at some point she must have fallen asleep. He prayed she was asleep. One of them needed some rest, and Slade knew that until Jessie was his again, rest would be only a dim memory.

He faced a battle in getting Jessie back and he knew it. Jazz and the others would stand aside, not so much because they wanted to, more because he had no intention of backing down. Life had been a living hell every minute he had spent away from Jessie. He wasn't staying away from her now.

The thought of that separation was a separate, aching bitterness inside him. He had done his part for his country and destroyed his own happiness in the process. Through the grief and his determination to complete the operation as quickly as possible, he hadn't paid enough attention to the danger Amy was involving herself in. She was supposed to be his backup, his marriage was his ticket into the organization, but Amy had wanted more. She had seen it as a means to the power and the money he hadn't known she craved. It was a hunger he had overlooked right until the night her lover took them over an embankment and killed them both. The same night Kingston and Baines had been arrested.

Slade had nearly died that night. It had been Amy's job to call in the backup team of agents when he got into trouble. Instead, Amy was no place to be found. She had warned her lover, and with his help stolen nearly a million dollars in cash before attempting to escape.

The only person who cried at her funeral had been Cody. He was barely four, and though Amy hadn't been the best mother, she had been all Cody had known. Slade sighed wearily, shaking his head at the thought of his boy. Cody might not have his blood, but he was still his kid. He had raised Cody, loved him, given up his soul in the operation that had conceived him. He couldn't let him go.

How would Jessie feel about him though?

He dragged himself from the chair, slipped out onto his balcony before jumping the short distance to Jessie's. There, he unlocked the balcony door again, punched in the code to the alarm and then stood staring at her, soaking in the sight of the woman who had tormented him for five years.

He couldn't stay this morning, he had to head back to Amy's parents house and check on Cody before heading out to the house he had kept when he left town. The place needed opening and airing out before he and Cody moved into it.

Stepping carefully through the room, he only meant to check on her, but when he stepped to the bed, he felt the pain that wracked his chest. She was wearing that fucking shirt and sweat pants he had given her to wear home five years before. Both were faded with age, holes had been worn in the knees, but they wrapped around her, holding her as he couldn't.

She was lying on top of the blankets, her cheeks flushed, her pink lips parted and her dark hair spread around her head like a halo. Damn, she was prettier than ever. A soft, sexy little kitten that fit his body perfectly.

Slade knelt beside her, careful not to awaken her, his fingers moving to that glorious spread of hair, feeling its softness, luxuriating in the silken feel of it. He was a weak man. He had known that years ago when he had been forced to walk away from her. He had gotten the hell out of Loudoun as fast as he could, knowing that if he stayed much longer he would risk both their lives.

But God, he had missed her. Losing her had been like losing a limb, losing his soul. It had torn a hole through his spirit that still bled with pain, with aching hunger. But he was back now, and Jessie belonged to him. Fuck Jazz, Zack, Ron and whoever else thought they could keep him away from her. He had lived on dreams of her, on aching fantasies and the prayer that he would return to her.

He leaned toward her, his gaze captivated by her lips, drawn to her more now than he had ever been before. While she slept, her lips parted as she breathed deeply, he allowed his own to feather over them. Pillowy satin. Damp heat. The moan he held back shuddered through his body as he let himself settle further against her, kissing her like the treasure she was, the need for control tearing his muscles apart.

Until her lips parted further. A soft moan welled from her throat as she turned to him, her arm curling around his neck.

"Slade." The whispery sigh shattered his control.

His tongue slid past her lips, tangled with hers, and for the first time in five years he knew life. Heat exploded inside his body, pouring to his cock, hardening it instantly as her hand curved behind his neck while the other went searching for his abdomen. His hands clenched in her hair as he fought for his sanity, to confine his caresses to the kiss alone. And the kiss itself was paradise. They sipped at each other, lips, tongues and barely contained moans feeding into each other until Slade found himself stretched out on the big bed with her, holding her close as the taste of her filled his senses.

He licked at her lips, pulling back just enough to allow her little pink tongue to follow him, to lick back at him, to sink inside his mouth as a growl of need tore from his throat. His hands were beneath the shirt, shaping one firm, nipple-hardened breast while her hand tugged at his shirt, fought with his belt and her hunger grew.

He could feel it, with each second the kiss grew deeper, her hands more frantic until she finally tore the belt loose and began to struggle with his jeans. His cock was throbbing in anticipation, his muscles tense, so tight they ached as he fought to hold back. But she was so sweet, like nectar, like the soft warm syrup he knew was gathering on her pussy.

Did she still wax? The thought had his hands trembling as he restrained the need to check and see. She was still more asleep than awake. He should be shot for taking advantage as he was, for letting her fingers tear open the snap to his jeans, lower the zipper and reach in for the thick erection straining beneath his underwear.

His tongue plunged forcefully into her mouth as her fingers wrapped around the heated shaft. His thumb and forefinger plucked at her nipple as the other hand tugged at her hair until her head fell back and he lost himself in her.

He was only barely aware of his hands jerking at the sweatpants moments later, pushing them over her thighs as she fully released his straining cock. They were twisting against each other, lips stealing any protest she could have thought to make, though he was fairly certain the nails digging into his back had nothing to do with rejection and everything to do with the lust building between them.

He kicked his sneakers from his feet as her hands jerked and pulled at his jeans. Frantic cries were echoing in her throat as he finally managed to get one of her sweetly shaped legs free. The damp heat of her pussy pulled at him almost as desperately as her fingers did.

"Jessie," he groaned her name, his lips moving to her neck. "For God's sake. Wake up. Wake up, baby."

"Fuck you. Let me sleep." She was moving beneath him as he moved over her, her hands pushing his shirt out of the way as he felt the buttons tearing from the one she wore. "Finish it. Don't leave me hurting again, Slade. For God's sake, finish it this time."

She was awake. Her eyes were dark slits, staring up at him. He moved between her thighs, his cock nudging, sliding through the slick cleft of her pussy as her thighs parted for him.

Slade gritted his teeth, positioned himself at the entrance and began to push inside her. She was tight. He stared down at her, watching her expression as she struggled to take him, feeling her hips lift, writhe beneath his. She gasped, her head tossing on the pillow while he pushed in further.

"You're as tight as you were the first time, baby girl," he growled. "Sucking at my dick like a hungry little mouth."

Her cheeks flushed further as her pussy grew slicker.

"You like that, don't you, baby? That little bit of pain biting into your cunt." He pushed deeper inside her, lowering one arm to lift her leg higher along his hips, hearing her whimpering cry as the tight little muscles struggled to take him.

"There, sweet baby," he whispered. "Tell me what you want. You want me to take you bit by slow bit? Or do you want it all at once? Tell me, baby. Do you want more heat?"

"More..." Her cry had his teeth clenching. "Oh God, Slade. Take me hard. I want it all..."

She arched as he slid back, then her scream echoed around him when he tore inside her with one hard, furious stroke. He stilled, embedded in her to the hilt, his head falling to the pillow at her shoulder. He felt the delicate tissue ripple around him, enclose him, suckling him with a firm, ultra-tight grip that had his balls drawing up tight to the base of his cock.

"God, you're hot." He bit at her shoulder then licked the little wound as her hands scratched at his back. "So hot and sweet." He pulled back slowly, an inch at a time, relishing the flex and clench of her pussy as she fought to hold him inside her. "Want to do it again, baby? Hard and deep?"

"Again." She was panting, her hips jerking as he felt her tightening beneath him, reaching for her orgasm.

He chuckled hoarsely. "Close, aren't you, baby girl? One more hard push will do it for you, won't it?"

He didn't give it to her. He worked his cock inside her instead, his hips pushing, twisting, his erection digging into the clenched tissue as she moaned and cried beneath him. She was as fist-tight, as hot and desperate as a virgin. She may have taken a lover, but she hadn't found what only he could give her. What he had taught her to take from his body alone.

"Look at me, Jessie," he growled as her eyes closed. "Look, baby." He reared back on his knees, lifting her hips as he pulled back. His cock dripped with her juices as her eyes focused, widened and he felt her pussy clutching harder at the head of his cock. "There you go. Watch me take you, sweetheart. Watch and know who this sweet little body belongs to."

He slid in slowly, watching as the soft folds parted for the thick shaft sinking inside her. He was forced to clench his teeth against the pleasure, the need to fuck her until they were both screaming in release.

But he couldn't. Not yet. In this moment he had to reinforce the knowledge that she belonged to him. Only him.

"Don't torture me, Slade." Her plea nearly broke his control. "Oh God, please fuck me. Please..."

"Easy, baby." He was embedded to the hilt again, his balls pressing against the curves of her ass as her clit peeked out, swollen and pink. He stared down at the point where he possessed her, feeling her milking his cock, aching to come.

"You have the sweetest pussy," he whispered, watching as he pulled out again, grimacing in painful pleasure at the sight of her cream coating his cock. "Slick and hot and so tight. I want to savor every stroke, Jessie. Savor it, baby. Let it build. Remember how much better it is when we wait."

He remembered. Remembered watching her, just like this, in his bed, as he fucked her for nearly an hour, making her wait until both of them were pouring with sweat, until his cock was an agonized shaft of pure sensation.

"I've waited enough," she panted, her breathing harsh, her breasts rising and falling with the effort it took to drag air into her lungs. "I've waited forever, Slade."

"Just a little bit more." His hand pressed against her lower belly as he forced his cock inside her again, feeling her womb spasm beneath his hand. "You can wait just a few more minutes, baby. Let me feel you like this, tight and hot, wrapping around me like molten silk. Oh yeah, suck me with that tight little pussy, sweetheart. Suck my cock until neither of us can stand it anymore."

The violent spasms ripping through her cunt were killing him as he retreated, stopping until only the thick head remained, watching her clit swell, redden.

"Again," she moaned. "Go in again, Slade. Oh God, stretch me. Make it burn more."

His hips jerked, driving his erection several inches inside her, almost triggering the climax she was reaching for so desperately.

"Bad girl." He lifted one hand from her hips, delivering a sharp little slap to her ass that only had her cunt creaming more.

She jerked in his grip, a desperate cry falling from her lips as her pussy sucked harder at the head of his cock.

"Whose pussy is this?" He pressed the flat of his palm against her clit, pumping it gently as he watched her eyes daze from the need to orgasm. "Give me what I want, Jessie, and I'll let you come. Tell me whose pussy this is. Who has it missed, baby? Who owns this tight little cunt?"

"No..." She wailed in protest. "No games, Slade. Please..."

"Tell me." He pumped inside her hard and deep, forcing himself to stop as he felt her begin to peak.

"You bastard!" she screamed, her fists clenching in the quilt beneath her.

"Tell me." He rubbed at the little clit with the pad of his palm, determined, set on this one small admission. "Tell me, damn you. And no lies. Lie to me, Jessie and I'll stop. You can give this tight little pussy to only one man, damn you. Now who the fuck does it belong to?"

"You!" Her strangled scream was thick with tears. "Goddamn you, it belongs to you..."

His control snapped. He came over her, his hips thrusting, pounding his cock into her. He felt her shatter beneath him, felt her pussy tighten and weep as he fought himself to pull back, to pull out and spill his seed to the mattress rather than the rich depths of her convulsing womb.

She was trembling beneath him as he collapsed over her, barely catching his weight with his elbows. She shuddered with the aftershocks of her pleasure, hard tremors racing over her body for long seconds. She was warm, soft, and for a moment, just a moment, he could pretend he had never lost her.

Chapter Twelve

"Get out," Jessie screamed as she threw Slade's shoes at him while he cinched his belt, watching her with lazy satisfaction. "And don't bother coming back. The next time you show up here I'll call the police."

He grabbed the other shoe a second before it connected with his head. He sat down on the bed, untying them and pushing his socked feet unhurriedly into the sneakers.

"You act like I raped you," he grunted. "You were the one tearing at my jeans..."

"Shut up." She had discarded the shirt and sweats, pulling on a robe and belting it tightly around her waist instead. "Just shut up and get out."

"Are you on the pill?"

"None of your damned business. Get out."

"It would have been if I came inside you like I wanted to," he growled. "Watch out, baby, or you might get caught more effectively than you want."

"Women have been having babies for years without the moron fathers tagging along," she informed him, her voice furious.

"Not mine." His head snapped up, his gaze suddenly sharp, fierce. "Never a kid of mine, Jessie, and you know it. Not if I can help it."

He had been abandoned as a child, raised in one foster home after another until he escaped and headed to college. He had always sworn he would never leave a kid of his to suffer as he had.

Jessie shook her head, weary to her very soul as she faced him.

"You should carry condoms, stud. The way you fuck around, you'd think they would be second nature," she snapped.

He didn't say a word. He laced his shoes then rose from the bed, towering over her as she backed away from him.

"If you're not on birth control then get on it," he growled. "Condoms break, Jessie."

Well, that put her in her place.

"Yeah, you wouldn't want your little river slut getting knocked up," she sneered furiously.

"Enough." He gripped her arms, a quick little shake leaving her to stare up at him in shock. "Never call yourself something so vile again or I'll paddle your ass until you can't sit down for a week. I never thought of you that way."

"Then you should have." She jerked away from him, moving out of the bedroom and heading to the kitchen. "You've had your morning fun, now you can get the hell out."

She fought the trembling of her hands, but nothing could erase the lazy satisfaction in her body. Slade had taken her not just once, but twice. Taking her until she couldn't move, couldn't even cry out, she could only come, over and over again, washing his hard cock with her release each time he demanded it.

She was pathetic. As though he hadn't already walked away from her once, she had to fall at his feet and beg him to do it again.

"Jessie." His voice stopped her as he followed, darker, deeper than she had ever heard it.

She turned back, facing him as self-disgust, fury, and her own pathetic needs washed over her.

"I love you."

She blinked back at him in shock.

"What?"

His expression was stoic, resigned, his eyes nearly black as he watched her.

"I love you now, and I loved you then," he whispered, his voice harsh. "As God is my witness, if I could have found another way..." He swallowed tight, glancing away from her before straightening his shoulders and facing her once again. "If I could have, I would have done things different."

She couldn't handle this. She lifted her hand, moving away from him before walking to the door and pulling it open with a quick, violent jerk.

"You're not going to do this to me again." She couldn't look at him, she stared into the hallway, watching the fingers of sunlight wash over it, piercing the fog as the pain she had pushed back years ago began to pierce her heart. "Don't come back, Slade. Not for any reason."

She heard him breathe deeply as he neared her, felt his warmth as it washed over her, once again warming that place in her heart that had been cold for so long. She steeled herself against it. Slade was a liability to her, and she knew it. He was a weakness she couldn't afford.

"Jessie?" His voice throbbed, the sound of it as agonized as the well of heartache opening inside her.

She turned back to him, staring into the somber, saddened expression that filled his face.

"It doesn't go away. I thought it would. I thought I could do what was right and live with the decision. I thought I could be strong." A bitter smile shaped his lips. "I learned better."

He stepped past her, moving into the hall. She watched him go, breathing in with jerky breaths, her lips tightening to hold back the tears as she closed the door quietly behind him. He wouldn't stay away, and she knew it. He believed what he was saying, just as she believed nothing could change the past.

Shaking her head, she moved through the living room to the kitchen and sat down in one of the chairs as a frustrated groan left her lips. What the hell was she supposed to do now? She had spent too many years getting over Slade to let him walk back in and mess up her heart and her head again. Too many years spent trying not to cry, not to give up because it hurt so bad she just wanted to hide.

She was not going to let him do this to her.

His pussy? She didn't think so. She may have faltered in her sleep, but there were ways to keep that from happening ever again, and she would make certain he didn't get the opportunity. He could ambush her when she was dreaming of him, but if he couldn't get to her, then he couldn't ambush her.

She smiled, cold determination filling her. Slade was going to learn that she wasn't the pushover he obviously thought she was.

* * *

Jessie was going to play hard to get.

For the first time in five years, Slade felt the blood pumping through his body, anticipation surging through his system. A smile curved his lips. The first one since that weekend he had spent with Jessie, a true smile, filled with amusement, warmth and joy.

Damn, she had always had the ability to do that, to fill him with a challenge, even though he knew she was his. It was a rare woman who had the ability to challenge a man even though he knew he already had her. And Slade knew he had her. She could rage and fight and argue until hell froze over, but she was his, and he would prove it.

She wanted to play first, that was fine. He could handle a little playtime. The sharp edge of hunger had been blunted that morning as he filled her, as he heard her screams echoing around him and felt her pussy spasm around his dick. He'd spent two days, five years ago, teaching her to match his body, his hungers. He didn't care what she wanted to convince herself of, no one else would ever do for either of them.

For now, he sat in the runabout, stretched out in the bench seat at the back, hiding in the shadows as he watched the party on the bank. He had pulled in late, beaching the small craft and searching out Jessie's form. He had found her quickly, chasing about the firelight with Rhonda, obviously taking her shift at childcare.

She was a natural, eagle-eyed, quick, keeping the kids laughing and amused even as she kept them out of trouble. Snacks were set out beneath the awnings of the parked RVs, hot dogs and marshmallows were being roasted over the fires, and through it all, Slade watched her like the living, breathing dream she was.

He imagined her heavy with his child, a smile on her face as another child tagged behind her. She was a natural mother and, for a second, the need to tie her to him, to fill her with his babies was overwhelming.

Fuck, he was no better than Amy. He couldn't and he wouldn't trap Jessie like that, but damn, she had been made to be a mother, created with such a core of nurturing, healing love, that he couldn't imagine her not having his babies. His babies. Not Jazz's, and by God, sure as hell not any other man's. His.

He lifted his beer to his lips, drinking deeply as he contented himself with just watching her. It was enough, for now. Seeing her joking with Momma Rhonda, the little spitfire who ruled the parties held here as any mother ruled a family. Ron stood not far away, always near his wife, always watching her, even when a man thought he wasn't. He was prone to overindulge, but even falling down drunk he watched his wife with a possessiveness Slade hadn't understood, until he found Jessie.

"You gonna come up here or hide all night?" Zack stepped from the shadows and stared at Slade mockingly.

"I'm just watching." Slade lifted his beer before tipping it to his mouth once again, his eyes never leaving Jessie. "Damn, Zack. I missed this."

And he had. The camaraderie, it was different here. He maintained a distance as an agent with the various skirmishes ranging to hell and back. He'd lost enough friends, he couldn't face losing friends like Zack or Jazz, so he hadn't made any others.

"Yeah well, you might have been missed a bit too." Zack jumped to the runabout, moving to the swivel seat in front of Slade as he plucked a beer from the ice chest on the floor and twisted the cap free. "We worried 'bout ya, man. That was some serious shit you were into. I saw the news story when the stories of the arrests broke. It wasn't pretty."

Slade sighed tiredly. "No, it wasn't." He kept his eyes on Jessie, as he had kept her in his mind during those hellish years.

He let a smile tip his lips as he watched Jessie's gaze rove over the shoreline. She couldn't see the boat, or him. A frown marred her brow a second before she turned back to the kids, laughing with a chubby little toddler as he waved a burned marshmallow up at her.

"We worried 'bout her too," Zack finally said, his voice quiet. "She wasn't the same. Worked too much. She bought the RV as soon as it went up for sale, going through Jazz to hide it from you, then renting your apartment. It seemed to ease her some, so we let it go. But we worried."

Not as much as Slade had. He had known Jessie was buying it, had priced it ridiculously low for that simple fact.

"You weren't alone, Zack." He flicked his gaze toward his friend before it was drawn once again to Jessie. "You know why I did what I had to do. I didn't have a choice. I did it the only way I knew how."

"Yeah." He saw Zack's abrupt nod from the corner of his eyes. "I thought we were buddies though. You could have told me."

"I didn't tell her." He tipped the beer toward Jessie as she swung another youngster into her arms. "And she holds my soul."

Zack snorted. "You're waxing poetic, man."

Slade laughed at the accusation. "She's worth it. Watch her. Son of a bitch, I don't think I've ever seen anything so pretty in my life."

"Man, you're just eat up with it," Zack groaned. "I hope it's not contagious. So what are you gonna do, just sit here and watch her all night? Or ambush her like you did this morning?"

Slade swung his gaze back to Zack.

"You think no one would hear her screaming like a dying banshee?" He laughed. "Hell man, I work the office on Saturday. You two had me sweating down there."

Slade wiped his hand over his chin, grinning back at the other man in unabashed amusement.

Zack chuckled, a thread of exasperation running through his voice. "She's not going to be that easy to pull in, boy. Sideswiping her ain't gonna gain you any points either."

Slade shrugged, finished his beer and reached for another.

"I can wait. I waited five years."

"And Jazz? He's taken care of her, Slade. Maybe he's not ready to let her go."

"Don't remind me of that black-hearted, woman-thieving, poor excuse for a grinning fool," Slade snapped furiously. "He's lucky I didn't cut his dick off for touching her. And don't start with the Goddamned maybes either. I've had enough of those out of him."

He still wasn't certain he shouldn't whip Jazz's ass again. The only thing that saved the overgrown jackass was the fact that Jessie had come apart in *his* arms, her pussy so snug she nearly strangled his cock, her eyes dazed, the shock and surprise at the pleasure tearing through her proof enough that Jazz hadn't touched her heart. He hadn't touched what mattered. The rest Slade would forgive. In time.

"So what do you intend to do? Watch her until she breaks?" Zack snickered back at him.

Slade lifted his brow in amusement. "A good agent learns fast when to watch and when to strike, remember that, Zack? She knows I'm here, she knows I'm watching. I'll know when to strike."

Chapter Thirteen

What the hell was he up to?

Monday afternoon, Jessie lay on the balcony outside her bedroom, listening to Jazz, Zack and Slade's voices as they argued over something in the apartment he had tortured her by moving into. Dammit, they had an office, why the hell didn't they take it there instead of interrupting her summer? Besides the fact they wouldn't argue loud enough for her to hear it.

She frowned, catching only scattered words, never a phrase or an inkling to what the debate was over. Her curiosity was driving her crazy. And Jazz, damn him, probably knew it.

The office building itself was back from the main road and fairly private. With the towels she used to cover her balcony rails, she was hidden from view below, allowing her to sunbathe nude whenever she wanted to, as she was now. It was a hazard, because the sound of Slade's voice was making her horny.

Realizing she was once again caressing her abdomen and moving much too close to the waxed folds between her thighs, Jesse flipped back to her stomach. The murmur of Slade's voice was driving her crazy.

At this rate, masturbation wasn't far away and she refused to allow his voice to push her to that point. No matter how good it would be.

It would be easier if she could actually hear him acting like an ass! A frown creased her brow at the fierce thought, even as she snorted at herself in derision. It was a damned lie. Slade's voice, whether pissed off or sexually determined, had the power to make her pussy gush with the need to fuck. The feel of him sliding into her, stretching her, setting her on fire, was one of the things she had never been able to forget. Even Jazz couldn't do that to her. The prickling lash of erotic pain at penetration had been more uncomfortable than pleasurable when he had taken her. With Slade, she only craved more.

"You're going to burn."

Speak of the devil. Jessic turned her head, meeting Jazz's laughing eyes as he stepped onto Slade's balcony. He raised and lowered his brows in lecherous regard as his eyes went over her nude body.

If Monday was starting out this bad, then the rest of the week could only get worse.

Sitting up, Jessie jerked the light wrap from the floor of the balcony and pulled it over her head before facing him again.

"Shouldn't you be building something?" she grumped, rising to her feet before moving to the small ice chest she had filled with drinks earlier. She jerked a bottle of water from the cold interior before slamming it closed again.

"Eh, that's what I pay my hands to do." He shrugged negligently. "So I can play when I want to."

The white T-shirt he wore stretched over his broad chest, emphasizing his lean hips and hard abs before disappearing into the band of his jeans. He was still wearing his boots, which gave his powerful legs a sexy, alpha look. There were days she wished she had fallen in love with the gentle giant rather than the brooding asshole she had given her heart to when she was sixteen years old.

"Slug." She grinned as he braced his hand on the railing before jumping over it and landing on her balcony.

"Hell, a man has to take time to enjoy the fruits of his labors." He smiled back at her, tipping the straw cowboy hat back on his thick head of hair as he settled himself into the padded chair beside her and accepted the beer she handed him. "Besides, I wanted to check up on you. You were too quiet Saturday night."

She had been a nervous wreck. She felt Slade watching her, his eyes following her every move. He had been no place to be seen, but she could feel him.

She shrugged at the question, drinking her water rather than discussing Slade.

"He's changed, huh?" Jazz finally said. "Not as easygoing as he was."

"He always had it in him." She threw him a quick look. "Don't play games with me, Jazz, we both knew Slade was always too sure of himself, too arrogant. It just wasn't as developed then."

He nodded. "Sometimes it just takes a powerful force to strip a man down like that..."

"Don't you start on me." She flashed him a hard glare. "I don't want to hear it, I don't want to know. Slade is a part of the past and he's going to stay there. I told you Friday night, I don't want to hear your lectures and I mean it."

He sighed, aggravation reflecting on his strong-boned face.

"Slade's not in the past anymore, Jess. He's right here now, and he's set his sights on you again. And sorry, sweet pea, you lost your own bet. You gave in."

She flushed at the reminder. Anyone in the office below the other morning had heard her screams. The bastard. He had made certain of it.

"Doesn't mean a thing." She rolled the cold water bottle between her palms. "He won't ambush me like that again. I'm having the locks changed on the doors and security codes changed..."

"And you think that's going to stop Slade?" He was laughing at her now. "Baby, you forget what he's good at. Security is Slade's specialty. Why do you think him and Zack are fighting like two polecats determined to mark their territory now? He doesn't like our security or the company we use. He's getting ready to overhaul the whole damned thing. He'll ghost right past your puny little alarms."

She lifted a lip in a silent sneer. "I'll have him arrested."

"For what? Making you scream in heat?" Yes, he was laughing at her. Enjoying the predicament she was finding herself in.

"When you finally fall in love, I hope it's the bitch from hell," she snarled. "I hope she works your guts into so many knots you can't think straight."

He opened his eyes wide. "I think straight now?"

Her shoulders drooped in defeat, her head dropping as she shook it in resignation. There was no making sense with Jazz. He didn't have any sense. She was certain he was nothing but a little boy in a grown man's hard-packed body. Damned nice packaging, but hell if he knew how to do anything but tease and torment the rest of the world.

As she opened her lips to speak, a movement from the corner of her eyes caught her attention. She was cursed. It was just that simple. A second later Slade hauled himself over the heavy rail of his balcony and stepped over the distance to hers, his gray eyes slicing toward them, his body tense, hard, as he stared at Jazz.

"Why not just build a fucking walkway between the balconies?" she snapped. "Before someone breaks their damned neck."

What was it about jeans and boots that just made a man too sexy to look at? Combine it with the white button-down shirt and the brooding anger on Slade's face and her pussy was creaming. Furiously. Her clit throbbed as anticipation surged through her even as anger burned inside her chest.

"What do you want?" She glared at him, hating the way her body reacted to him, how everything inside her woke up and started screaming his name.

"Have lunch with me." He didn't beat around the bush. "We'll take the bike into the mountains and talk."

Talking was the last thing on his mind if that bulge beneath his jeans was anything to go by.

"Hey there, Slade, you're not going to say hi to me?" Jazz's booming voice caused Jessie to wince. She could hear the challenge in it. "Slade ain't talked to me all day. He's being right unsociable, sweet pea."

Slade didn't even look at Jazz, he continued to stare at Jessie, his expression forbidding, reminding her of the warning he had given her the other morning.

"Can you believe this?" Jazz grumped. "Son of a bitch loosens my teeth for me and then can't even say howdy two days later. My best girl won't talk to me, and my favorite cow tried to stomp my feet. I'm tellin' ya'll, Mercury must be in retrograde again."

"Shut up, Jazz," she muttered, the look in Slade's eyes making her nervous.

"Shut up, hell," he retorted, flashing Slade a hard smile. "Bastard goes riding off for five fucking years without even a 'by your leave' and thinks he can just walk right in and own the world again. Maybe I want to keep my little stake in it."

Slade growled.

Jessie jumped to her feet, wedging herself between the two of them. "I've had enough of this. Take it somewhere else, both of you. Go kill each other for all I care but you're not doing it on my balcony. Get off."

"You wouldn't let me, remember?" Jazz flashed her a wicked smile as Slade took a warning step forward, his hands gripping her arms to move her to the side.

Jessie stared at Jazz incredulously. "Have you lost what little mind you used to own?" she asked carefully.

"Maybe." He tipped the beer to his lips, swallowing in a lazy movement as he winked back at her flirtatiously. "You'd be worth being senseless for, sweet pea."

"Jessie." Slade's voice was darker, more dangerous than she had ever heard it. And warning. She glanced at him, her lips thinning at the dangerous tension that marked his expression.

"Fuck it. Kill each other. See if I care." She stomped around Slade, glancing at the balcony where Zack stood watching the scene in amusement.

"Would you care to make sure they don't kill each other on my damned balcony?" she snarled. "And unless you want your security boy locked in jail for the week, keep him out of my damned apartment." Evading Slade's hand as he reached out to her, Jessie pushed her way into the apartment and slammed the glass door closed behind her.

"Jessie." Slade's voice was furious through the door, not that she really cared at that point. She could have cheerfully taken a bat to both of them right then. It was like dealing with two little over-spoiled children.

Jerking a cami and shorts from her dresser, she grabbed her sneakers from the floor and stalked to the bathroom for a shower. A cold shower. The more she fought with Slade, the more aroused she had become. He was killing her, destroying her control and her will and she had no idea how to fight it.

Half an hour later, dressed, furious and aching, she left her apartment, heading for the stairwell when the door opened and Slade stepped into the hallway.

"Where the hell do you think you're going?" His expression was dark, his gray eyes glittering with lust and suppressed anger. She moved to push past him, determined to ignore him. She found herself plastered to the wall instead, pulled from her feet. Slade's aroused body held her pinned to the wall. Jesse felt lightning flare through her clit, a heated kick of sensation spearing her womb as he pressed his jeans-covered erection into the notch he forced between her thighs.

"Your pussy's fucking wet," he growled, his eyes thunderclouds of lust. "Your nipples are hard and your face is flushed, I bet I could sink inside you now and you'd glove me like a silken fist. So why are you running?"

"Let. Me. Go." She held herself stiffly, her nails biting into his powerful forearms as she glared at him.

His hips pressed tighter, stealing her breath at the caress to her clit. Oh God, if he did that many more times, she was going to come.

"Don't run from me, Jessie." His voice was a guttural throb. "We both know it's not going to work. We can start over—"

"Like hell," she snarled back in his face, shaking with the force of the anger surging through her. "For God's sake, Slade. You've been gone five years. Five fucking years. Did you think I was going to just lie here pining for you and wait for you to bring that big overconfident dick of yours back into my life?" she snapped insultingly. "Do you think because my body likes how you touch it that that's all it's going to take to turn me back into the stupid little girl I was then?" She struck out at his shoulders with her fists, bucking against him, snarling when he refused to let her go.

"Shush." The fingers of one hand gripped her hair as the growl vibrated between them. He held her in place easily. "You'll be my sweet little Jessie," he whispered, staring into her eyes, stealing her breath with the depth of emotion in his gaze. "Yes, baby, you are my sweet little treasure. All mine. That tight little pussy, your smart little mouth, and that tender heart you think you can hide from me." His hips rotated against hers. "All mine."

His lips brushed hers and she was almost lost. Almost.

"No!" She jerked to the side, forcing her legs down, stumbling away from him as she fought to steady her breathing.

Hard hands helped right her, but they weren't Slade's. Jazz and Zack were there, catching her as she stumbled. She jerked away from them, staring at them in fury, in pain. He was going to kill her. He was breaking her heart, pushing for the one thing she was most terrified of—giving him her heart again. Losing him again would kill her and she knew it.

"Moron." Her voice was thick with tears. Emotions tore through her, feelings she had hidden even from herself while he had been gone. Things she didn't want to feel, didn't want to destroy her again. "Can't you understand this is over?" she cried. "You left me, Slade. I didn't leave you and I won't let you destroy me again."

She moved quickly from the three of them, walking furiously toward the parking lot and freedom. If she didn't get away from him, she was going to break. She was going to lose her heart, her senses and her mind and that terrified her.

Slade watched her leave, tenderness swelling inside him even as his heart clenched at the pain he saw in her face. God, she had grown, become stronger, surer. She wasn't going to fall into his arms. His Jessie had a backbone that was stiff as steel and despite the fact that he knew, to the bottom of his soul he knew, she still loved him, she wasn't willing to give in yet.

"She's going to shoot your ass before it's over with." Jazz shook his head as Slade glanced at him. The other man's expression was pitying, his gaze filled with resignation. "I don't think I've ever seen Jessie that damned mad. You make her cry and she's going to rip your eyes out, Slade. You know that about her. She's been like that since she was a kid."

That wasn't anger. It was pain, confusion, a woman fighting a battle she had no hope of winning. That's what Slade knew. For a second, one pulse pounding, hotter than hell second, she had been his, her body relaxing, melting into him, ready for him. He had seen it in her eyes, felt it in the soft curves that pressed against his erection.

She wasn't pissed; she was scared. Scared and running. There was a difference.

"She'll be okay." He flexed his shoulders, fighting the tension building there. "I'll make sure of it." He hadn't come back, he hadn't bet his soul on winning her back for nothing. For five years she had haunted him, cried out to him in his dreams and tortured him in his fantasies. She had been all that had kept him sane, and he had no intention of letting her go.

"Slade, man, do you know what the hell you're doing?" Exasperation echoed in Zack's voice.

"Hell no, he don't," Jazz chimed in. "He's like a bull in a china shop chasing a little mouse. He's going to break everything in his path."

"Starting with your numb skull," Slade bit out, the knowledge that his buddy had bedded his woman enraging him. "Don't push me, man. The only reason you're still alive is because she would likely shoot me herself if I killed you. Castration is still an option."

Jazz snorted. "Dickhead. Maybe she deserves better than you. Maybe I think I can take care of her a hell of a lot better than you've proved you're capable of."

"What the fucking hell is up with your goddamned maybes?" Slade yelled, his fists tightening with restrained rage. "Did you fry your fucking brain while I was gone?"

"Maybe." A wide grin split his face. "You have to admit, she's hot enough to do it..."

Slade jumped for him.

Chapter Fourteen

Jessie pulled into the shaded parking lot for Rigor Construction late that evening, checking carefully for any sign of Slade as she parked then slipped into the door that led to the stairs. He was making her paranoid, she thought as she unlocked the apartment door, checked her rooms quickly then tossed her packages to the bed. She closed the curtains over the balcony door and windows, letting the cool air of the air conditioner wash over her flushed flesh as she stripped.

She headed for the shower, flexing the tense muscles of her shoulders as she stepped into the bathroom. Adjusting the water, she moved beneath the spray and let it pound at the kinks in her back.

Slade was making her crazy. Another day or two of this and she was going to be a jabbering, horny idiot. A smile crossed her lips. Or maybe not. The toys she had purchased at the little store were going to have to help. The thick vibrating dildo wasn't Slade, but it should be relief. The anal toy and mini massaging Pocket Rocket hedged her bets that if she could get rid of the arousal, then she could hold out against Slade.

Finally clean, refreshed, she flipped off the water, dried her hair before wrapping a larger towel around her body and stepping from the bathroom. She glanced at her feet, considering her toes and a little girly pampering. Maybe a coat of scarlet polish. That would look good, give her a smidgen of added confidence maybe, she thought as she started to lift her head.

And she caught sight of the boots. Dark, scarred boots and frayed denim.

Jessie came to a stop, her heart racing as her chest tightened in feminine fear. Not physical fear—primal fear. The fear of a woman who knows she is caught. And she was caught. The bag from the toy store lay on the floor, the containers the toys had been sealed in had been opened.

Her gaze lifted over long muscular legs, a mouthwatering bulge that had her cunt screaming out in joy. Up, up, to the dark, lust-lined expression of the man she had never had the strength to resist. In one hand he held the dildo, in the other the anal wand.

He considered the wand for a long moment before shifting his gaze to hers. His gray eyes were nearly black in his hard face.

"Do you really think this is going to do it?" he asked. "That when you slip it up your tight little ass that it's going to give you what I did?"

She licked her lips nervously, suddenly terrified of what she knew he could and he would do to her.

"I asked you not to come back here."

God, how had he gotten in and she hadn't even known it? Hadn't heard him? She trembled, shaking with the hunger burning in her soul, the needs ripping through her. She had existed on autopilot for five years. Going through the motions, pretending, even to herself, that everything was okay. Now she was alive again and it was killing her.

He glanced at the wand.

"I remember how tight your little ass is." His voice was strangled. "How much you liked having it opened, having my cock sinking into it, making the pleasure hurt. Do you think this is going to make you hurt enough, Jessie?"

He stepped closer. Jessie retreated.

"Don't," she whispered, suddenly desperate, knowing she couldn't fight him as well as herself. "Don't do this to me, Slade. Please leave."

"I'm not Jazz, Jessie," he growled. "I won't walk away and I'll sure as hell not dangle on a string while you try to make up your mind. I've dangled on someone else's string for five fucking years. I'm pulling in the slack now, baby."

He picked up the tube of lubrication he had laid on the small bed table as he tossed the dildo to the chair in the corner of her bedroom. "You won't need that, darlin'. My cock is plenty good enough to still the fires in that sweet pussy. But this," he indicated the wand in his hand, "we can play with this a little." Her ass flexed, her anus tingling in response as she fought for the fury she knew should be burning inside her. All she could find was the arousal, the lust.

Yes, he had taught her body to crave him, just as he had declared. And it did crave. It hungered. It screamed with need, and finding the will to fight it was killing her. She retreated instead, moving back as he edged closer, his expression so dark, so intent, she felt the juices dripping from her pussy in response.

"I don't want you!" She stomped her foot furiously. "I hate you, Slade. Do you hear me?" She retreated further, the breath locking in her throat at the knowledge that he was pushing her closer to the bed.

"I hear you, baby," he crooned, his gray eyes gentling but no less filled with lust. "But you love what I do to you, don't you? You love how I can make you hurt and crave more of it. How the pleasure gets so fucking hot, you know you're going to burn and you jump right into the fire. That's what I'm going to do, Jessie. I'm going to show you all the things we both only dreamed of in the last five years."

"No, I didn't." Her fingers fisted in the towel as he crowded her nearer the bed. "I forgot about you the minute you left. I didn't even miss you."

She was shaking, she wanted him so badly. Trembling with the awareness that the clawing lusts that tortured her for years would be sated by his body, his hunger, his ability to still the needs that ravaged her even as he made her crave more.

He laid the wand and tube of lubrication on the small table by the bed before whipping his shirt off. He didn't argue, he didn't say a damned word. He undressed. Tossing his shirt to the side, his gaze never leaving her, he bent and removed the boots and socks before his hands went to the snap on his jeans.

"Drop the towel." His voice was graveled, thick with lust. "Let me see that pretty little body, baby."

"Go to hell!" she cried, shaking, anticipation tearing through her as the snap released and his finger went to the zipper.

Her mouth was watering. She remembered his taste, musk and male heat, the feel of his cock spurting into her mouth, his seed salty and rich as it attacked her taste buds before flowing down her throat. How many times had she dreamed of it, dreamed of feeling him between her lips, hearing his hard, explicit words as she sucked him dry?

"You should see your face." The zipper was open, his fingers hooking in the waistband before he shucked jeans and briefs, leaving his body gloriously naked. Straightening once again, his cock arrowed back from his abdomen, flushed with angry lust, the flared head damp with pre-come. "Such a hungry little baby," he crooned, his hand wrapping around the stalk. "Come here, baby. Come on, let me go crazy fucking your sweet mouth."

She whimpered. God, she was such a fool, a willing pathetic victim.

"Slade, please...I can't do this again..." She couldn't risk her heart.

"I lived for this," he whispered, his eyes tormented, his expression lined with an emotion that could have been pain. But why pain? He had left her, not the other way around. "I lived for the day I could come back here, that I could make up for what I did to you. That I could live again. I won't walk away, Jessie. You want it just as fucking bad as I do." He stepped closer. "We can do it the easy way, baby, or the hard way. Give me your sweet mouth."

His hand gripped the towel, pulling it away from her as she felt tears fill her eyes. She stared up at him, desperate, oh God, she was so desperate to taste him again, to take what he offered, to gorge herself on it.

"I hate you," she whispered.

"Of course you do, sweet baby." His hands pressed lightly on her shoulders as she sank to her knees. "And I don't blame you a bit... Fuck. Yes..."

Her tongue licked over the dark head, drawing in the taste of his pre-come, moaning at the intoxication of his passion. Her lips opened, wide, feeling his cock sink in as her hands gripped his powerful thighs and her senses stole reasoning.

"God. Baby girl." His hands threaded in her hair as his hips bucked against her lips, driving the crest deeper. "There you go, sweetheart. Love me, Jessie. Love me."

Instinct took over. There was no thought of the pain, the past receded and only the pleasure remained. She relaxed her throat, taking him deeper than she ever had before, swallowing against the thickness that threatened to strangle her before pulling back and repeating the process. Her tongue stroked against the underside of his cock as her hands moved, the fingers of the first cupping and stroking his taut testicles while the other moved to the cleft of his ass.

He jerked, forcing his cock deeper. She swallowed, moaned, her fingers finding the forbidden little entrance that brought such pleasure, and massaging slowly.

"That little fucker Jazz is dead," he groaned, a tortured sound of pleasure. "...fucking kill him...I know he taught you that. God. Fuck. You're killing me."

She let her throat stroke his crest as she massaged the anal entrance, her fingers cupping and tightening on his balls while her mouth tightened around his shuttling cock. Pre-come leaked furiously from the head, filling her with his taste as she gorged her senses on the fantasy come to life.

Animalistic growls echoed above her as his fingers bunched in her hair and pulled, creating a delicious burning tingle in her scalp that shot straight to her pussy.

"Yeah. There, baby, you go ahead..." he moaned roughly, a tortured sound of male pleasure as her fingers tormented him. "Tease, baby. Let me fuck that pretty mouth while you tease. Because you're going to scream..." He tightened to the breaking point as the tip of her finger pressed at the anal entrance. She massaged, teased; her throat swallowed against the head of his cock before it retreated, only to shuttle back.

"Hot fucking mouth," he groaned, pulling at her hair as she moaned in uncontrolled hunger. "I could live in your damned mouth, sucking my dick day and night... Oh baby... Sweet baby..." He was vocal. More vocal than she remembered him being as the explicit words filled her head, shook her senses.

She pulled her finger back from his ass, swiped it through the moisture that coated his cock before returning and entering the barest bit, pushing inside as he bucked against her. A shattered cry left his lips as hot, furious blasts of his come shot to her throat.

"God. Fuck. You little minx..." His voice was strangled as he flexed, a short little stroke that pushed his cock into the back of her mouth for each pulse of his semen before he jerked back from her.

Before she could gasp, he pushed her to the bed and jerked the tapered anal wand from the table. Slade rapidly coated it with lubrication before gripping her hand and wrapping her fingers around the hilt of it.

"Use it," he growled, staring at her like a man possessed by lust. "Spread your legs and fuck yourself with it."

She stared back at him, confused.

"Do it." He took her wrist, lowering it until the tip of the fake cock was nudging at the folds of her pussy. "Push it in. Let me watch you fuck yourself with it, Jessie. Let's see how hot you can get before I turn you over and fill your hot little ass with it. Play with me, baby."

Slade was shaking with lust, with love, with all the pent-up hungers and desires that had haunted him for far too many years. And there was the only reason he had stayed sane. Jessie. Her legs spread, her eyes staring up at him, innocence still reflected in the deep brown depths as he watched her press the tapered end of the anal wand into her tight little pussy.

She worked it in, gasping, filling his ears with the sweet sound of her greedy need as he watched the knobby length disappear up her pussy. The muscles of her thighs were tight, tense as her knees bent and her hips jerked against the intrusion. Her head thrashed on the bed as she whimpered his name.

Jazz might have taught her to suck cock, but he hadn't taught her this. She was as much a virgin to the toys as she had been to his cock the first time he filled her. And it was killing him. This was his shame, his insatiable lust for one delicate little woman, the need to push every sexual boundary she could possess as he stole her heart and soul for his own. Just as she owned his.

He had always had the power to make her want. He had seen that, been so brutally shocked by it when she was only seventeen that it had terrified him. The first time she orgasmed for him hadn't been in his RV that weekend. It had been on the bank of the lake, slow dancing, her bikini-clad breasts rubbing against his chest when he smartly slapped her ass for teasing him.

She had shuddered, her breath breaking, her face flushing as her eyes grew dazed and her hips bucked against him. It hadn't been much, hell, he doubted if she had known what had happened, but he had. And it had nearly killed him then not to take her. Waiting the next four years had been hell. The five years after he had first taken her had nearly killed him. And he intended to make up for it all now.

"God, that's pretty," he crooned, sitting on the bed below her, his hands settling on her knees to open her legs further. "Pull it back, baby, let me see you take your pretty pussy."

He watched the flushed, bare folds convulse at his words as her syrup bubbled from around the wand. He leaned forward, his tongue slowly licking around the shaft buried inside her, slurping the excess sweetness from the intimate lips.

"Go on." His hand at her wrist urged her on, his head pulling back, watching the toy sink inside her again. "Good girl. You keep doing that, baby, and I'll do this."

Picking up the lube, he spread a generous amount on his fingers. Lowering his head once again to the juice-laden curves, he tucked his fingers at the opening to her ass.

"Oh God. Slade..." Her hips lifted as he began to press two fingers into the tight entrance. He had no intention of easing her too gently into his return there. He wanted her to burn, wanted her to scream with the pleasure/pain he knew she craved.

"Did you miss me here, baby?" Thick, wide, he worked his fingers inside her, feeling her tissue spasm around them as her broken breaths filled the room. "Did you miss me up this sweet little ass?"

"Yes." The feminine growl had his cock jerking in its own demand. "Oh God, Slade, I missed you. I missed you bad."

Her hips arched, forcing more of his fingers inside her as whimpering cries left her lips.

"Here, baby." He brushed her still hand from the anal wand, knowing she had passed the point where she could fuck herself to completion with it. "Let's try this."

He pulled the toy from her pussy, eased his fingers from her ass despite her cry of protest. "Let me watch it fill your little ass."

He watched. Tucking it against the flexing entrance, he was consumed by the sight of her struggle to take each progressively larger knob until it was anchored in, no more than half the length disappearing up the little hole.

Her pussy was reddened, flowered open, the tender entrance fluttering in hunger. He shoved his tongue inside it, licking, suckling, consuming the sweetness flowing from it. She arched to him, a strangled scream leaving her throat as she began to orgasm from the hard thrusts of his tongue up the tight little portal.

He was a man possessed. Before the tremors eased from her, he was rising between her thighs, pulling the wand from her ass as he lifted her to him, pressing her knees back to her chest and positioning his cock to take what had remained his alone.

This was the final test of intimacy. Of giving. The trust it took to accept the intrusion here had always fascinated Slade. And no woman had ever taken him there with the hunger Jessie did.

The head popped in as she screamed beneath him, tensing at the sensations as he stretched her further than he had allowed the wand to stretch her. He spread her legs against his shoulders, his gaze going from her face to the impalement of her ass.

"I wish I had brought the dildo in here now," he growled. "I could push it inside your tight little pussy as I fill your ass. Would you like that, baby? Would you like me fuck you like that?"

Her head tossed, her eyes dark slits beneath her lowered lids as she panted for air.

"It hurts..." she whimpered, her ass flexing around him.

"Should I stop?" He moved to pull back, suddenly afraid he had pressed too far, too fast. God, sometimes it was hard to remember how tender she was, she took everything he gave her so readily.

"No," she cried out hoarsely. "Please don't stop...please..."

Her head moved back and forth as he felt the struggle to accept him in the spasming of her ass around the head of his erection.

"Do you like the pain, baby?" She liked the edge of pain. He knew that. Nothing severe, nothing extreme, just enough to make the pleasure sweeter.

"Yes," she gasped, finally easing around him enough to allow him to press forward.

"More?" He gave her another inch, hearing her cries as they shattered around him.

"More." She was fighting to breathe, her tummy tense, her clit flared to full life between the folds of her slit as she arched closer. "Oh God, Slade. I dreamed..." A tear trickled from her eye. "I dreamed of this. I dreamed and dreamed... Please. Please do it like you did before. Make me burn..."

His control was screwed. He jerked back, flipped her to her stomach before lifting her to her knees and returning to her. He worked his cock in, holding back, forcing himself to take her easier than his body demanded, working his shaft inside her until he filled her, stretched her, burned them both. Her back arched and her whimpering cries for more nearly shattered his control.

It wasn't easy. Not like it had been that first time. He was too hungry. Too deprived of the pleasure of her body. He fucked her like a man demented, digging into her ass with his cock with each thrust, growling, snarling, thrusting harder and deeper until he reached his hand beneath her, plumped her hard little clit and felt her shudder and pulse around him. His own release shot from his cock in blinding streams of hot come that had a shout erupting from his throat. He filled her, marked her, claimed her forever in each pulse of his orgasm as he collapsed over her.

For the first time in five years, the grieving pain in his chest lessened. It did nothing for his hard dick, though.

Chapter Fifteen

Jessie thought he would be finished. The violent orgasms that had torn through her body left her wasted on the bed. Unable to move, forget thinking, she drifted in a haze of satiation, certain that sleep was within seconds of arriving.

She hadn't been this tired in years; every bone and muscle in her body was relaxed, sated, weak as a newborn kitten. A smile edged her lips at that thought. Only Slade could do this to her, as much as she hated it.

She heard Slade in the bathroom, water running, something rustling. A second later the mattress dipped and he was filling her again, sliding into the swollen, still violently sensitive tissue of her pussy.

Her eyes widened, instantly caught by his gaze, his tender, cloudy gaze as his hands framed her face and a tight smile pulled at his mouth. The look in his eyes brought tears to hers. Heat and need, not sexual need, but a soul-deep, spirit-core hunger that she knew all too intimately herself.

"I'll be done soon." His breath broke as she spasmed around him, her hands moving to cover his, too tired to lift her arms to hold him to her. "I just want to hold you like this, feel you holding me. Hold me, Jessie." He rested his forehead against hers as she forced the energy into her tired arms to move.

She wanted to hold him. Forever. She wanted to feel the warmth of him seeping into her, the strength of him filling her. He was like a drug, one she was hopelessly, helplessly addicted to.

"Shush. No." His hands gripped hers, holding them against her head. "Not there. Here." He flexed his hips, pressing deeper, piercing her with a blinding wave of pleasure. "Just hold me, baby. Let me believe it's not just a dream."

The remnants of grief filled his eyes. Staring at him this close, her vision filled with the gray and black color, she watched the emotions that flickered in their depths.

"Slade." She protested the remorse she saw there. The possessiveness. "We can't go back..." Her breath broke as his hips flexed again, sending pleasure rushing through her. The engorged crest stroked over the entrance to her womb, pressing, sending flames leaping through the sensitive tissue.

"The past never left," he whispered, staring into her eyes. His hands moved to frame her face again, his thumb stroking over her lips as his expression twisted into lines of such amazing emotion it filled her soul with warmth. He warmed her. "The past has always been here..." He flexed inside her gently, heatedly. "And here..." He lowered his head, his lips pressing between her breasts, caressing the flesh over her rapidly beating heart. "It's never been gone, baby."

No, it hadn't been. It had lain inside her, sleeping, dreaming, waiting to awaken in Slade's arms. She knew that. Admitted it. There was no pleasure greater than this, nothing that could warm her from the inside out or fill the lonely places in her soul except Slade.

Tears filled her eyes as he moved inside her, his cock stroking through the tight muscles, slow and easy, sensitizing nerve endings that had lain dormant, awaiting his touch. God, she had missed him. She missed him like sunlight, like heat in the darkest winter. And like spring, the sunlight was back, warming her, cracking the ice and destroying the shields she had built against the pain.

"You left me." Her breath hitched at the remembered hurt as his body tightened above her. "You didn't want me..."

He jerked above her, his hands tightening on her head as his breath rasped from his chest.

"I wanted you more than I wanted to breathe." He raised his head, his hips moving against hers, stroking, stealing her mind, cementing her soul to his. "I wanted you until I ached, until my soul broke inside me, Jessie. And I couldn't have you. As much as I wanted you, I couldn't have you."

Why? She wanted to ask the question, wanted the answers but her body's wants overruled those of her heart. Her legs lifted, gripping Slade's hips as he began to fuck her with slow, easy strokes, the burning pleasure wiping through her senses and sending her spinning toward the sun.

Slow and easy. He didn't take her furiously, he didn't love her desperately. He loved her as he had that first weekend after the first blaze of lust had been fulfilled. He loved her with his lips on hers, his tongue tangling with hers, his hands holding her head still as he gave, and took only her pleasure in turn.

He loved her with his body, working his erection inside her gripping pussy, moaning at the clasp of her as she whimpered wordlessly at the heated stretching. He took her in ways she had never even dreamed of. Staring into her eyes, and as her orgasm washed over her, he lowered his lips to her ear.

"I'll love you until I die..." His body bucked above her as he whispered the words, his own release tearing through him, shuddering through his body and filling the condom she hadn't realized he had donned until that moment.

I'll love you until I die. So why had he left her and taken another woman with him?

Night had settled in, filling the interior of the bedroom with darkness as the curtains blocked the moonlight outside. Slade lay back on the bed, naked, his body covered by Jessie. She was stretched out on his chest, her hair falling down his side, her legs enclosed by his. A treasured weight that he relished as he listened to her breathe.

She had finally collapsed over him less than an hour before, shaking, exhausted by that final climax he had wrung from her straining body. He'd managed to hold onto her as he lifted her to his chest, disposed of the condom then lay back. It was then she sprawled over him, like a kitten determined to hold tight to the bit of territory it called its own.

His lips lifted in a grin as he played with her hair, lowered his head and kissed her forehead. He couldn't stay much longer. Amy's parents had heard the rumors that he was spending time with Jessie again and they were furious. Amy had fed her parents a malicious, bitter story of Slade's fascination with Jessie, and the failure of their marriage because of it. Damn, how had he missed the cold calculation in her? Or maybe he hadn't. He had known she hadn't been emotionally involved with him, it was one of the reasons he had accepted her as a partner on that case. He knew her. And he knew her heart wouldn't become involved. But her parents weren't aware of that.

He knew that before much longer, he wouldn't be able to trust them with Cody, he just hated jerking the boy away from them. Their last link to their daughter. But he wouldn't have Cody's young mind twisted by his grandparents either.

He didn't have much longer to secure Jessie's heart before he was going to have to tell her the truth, and he knew it. Hell, he should have already told her, should have been honest with her from the start rather than letting the years separate them. Hindsight was twenty-twenty and fucking vicious.

"You should be exhausted," she muttered against his chest, her voice drowsy, almost incoherent.

"And you are exhausted." He turned until he lay on his side, cuddling her close. "Go to sleep, baby. I have to get up in a bit and head out, I want to know you're dreaming of me when I go."

She stiffened in his arms, moving to pull away from him.

"I'm not stopping you..."

"No, you're not. I just get lazy as hell after loving you. I've been working on the house at night, trying to get it together again. Five years away and it needs a few repairs before I can move back into it. I'm ready to be home, Jess. It's been a long time."

"You never sold the house?" She plucked at the growth of hair on his chest, brushing her cheek over it as his body tightened in renewed need.

"You didn't have the money to buy it," he grunted. "You got my RV, baby. I figured that was enough."

"You knew I was buying the RV?" She frowned, staring up at him. "Jazz said you would never know."

Slade's gaze was hooded, brooding. "Jazz didn't need another fucking RV. That pervert lair is all he can handle. I knew who had it, who was living in it. You'd have had the house too if you wanted it."

Shock rifled through her as she shook her head in confusion. "You make as much sense as Jazz does anymore," she snapped. "If you cared so fucking much, why did you leave?"

And there was the crux of the matter. He had walked back into her life as though he belonged in it, as though she belonged to him. Not that she was achieving the fight she had always promised herself she would put up.

"We're going to discuss that one real soon." He sighed, his hand moving absently through her hair. "Not tonight, because there's just not enough time. But real, real soon, baby."

Real soon wasn't enough for her, he could see it in her eyes. She was getting past the pain and she was getting ready to demand answers. Those answers weren't going to be easy.

"You could sleep here." She stared up at him, her hesitancy obvious in her eyes. "We could talk."

Slade brushed her hair back, the back of his fingers prickling in pleasure at the feel of the silken strands.

"Not yet," he whispered gently. "Soon."

She wasn't concealing her hurt as easily as she thought she was. Moving back, she rose from the bed, drawing her robe over her naked body and belting it tightly.

"Whatever." She shrugged negligently, her pretense that it didn't matter biting into his anger, reminding him that he deserved it, even though he hated it. "It's up to you."

Slade suppressed his sigh. He couldn't leave Cody with his grandparents all night, as much as he wanted to. The weekends were hard enough. The boy worried incessantly when Slade didn't show up by bedtime, always concerned something had happened to his daddy, too.

He was going to have to explain things to Jessie. He had already waited too long, and he had no intention of hiding Cody.

He rose from the bed, gathering his clothes together. As he dressed, he listened to Jessie moving around the kitchen.

"I'll be by tomorrow..."

"I won't be here." She kept her head lowered as she opened the small chest freezer in the corner and pulled free a frozen Cornish hen. "School starts back in six weeks. I have to go up and start getting my room ready and I have shopping and stuff to do. I don't know what time I'll be home."

She was cool. Her hot little body was sated and she thought she could replace the distance between them. He didn't think so. He had worked too damned hard to get this far, spent too many sleepless nights dreaming of it. She wasn't going to push him away now that he was only beginning to feel the warmth of her heart once again.

"Then decide on a time." He pulled on his boots, watching her intently. "I want to see you before I have to go to the house tomorrow night. You're not hiding from me, Jessie, I don't care how much you want to."

She slammed the freezer closed and dumped the hen in the sink as she turned to face him.

"You don't own me, Slade." There was no anger in her voice, just pure steel. "I said I have things to do. Just as you have things to do. Don't try to storm your way over this because it won't work."

He glowered back at her, glimpsing the pure stubborn in her upraised chin. There was a time when she would have given in to him, when she would have waited for him. Those days were long gone he knew, but it was sure as hell hard to get used to this side of her. Not that he hadn't seen it growing in her before he left. She was one of those women who could scare you with just the glint of pure retribution in her eyes. So far, he had managed to avoid that. If he ever saw it, he was afraid he might just end up showing her how much power she did have over him.

Fine, she had work to do. He could work around that.

"I'll see you tomorrow anyway." He bent to kiss the frown on her forehead.

"I told you I won't be here," she snapped. "Do you ever listen to anything you don't want to hear, Slade?"

"Not anymore." He stalked toward the door, sliding it open as he glanced back at her. "And by the way, you're going to tell me you love me again soon, Jessie. I won't wait much longer."

"Don't hold your breath."

"I love you, baby."

"Kiss my ass, stud."

He left the apartment chuckling, realizing his heart was lighter than it had been in five years. She didn't have to say the words, he had the proof. And he wasn't going to take even a single chance that anything harmed it. Jessie was his.

Chapter Sixteen

She should have known he wouldn't let it go. Jessie was straightening the seats in the classroom assigned to her that year. Books were stacked on the floor, the shelves finally cleaned, though every other available surface was covered. The computer center was finally intact though, the six new computers installed and working perfectly as far as she could tell.

She was standing on one of the desks, stretching to the back of the final shelf as she tried to clear away the dust gathered in the corners when she felt hard hands grip her waist. She gasped, her hands clutching at the powerful wrists as she stared back at Slade.

A smile creased his lips, crinkled his eyes. One of the first she had seen since his return.

"Up you go, baby girl." He lifted her closer to the shelf as she took advantage of the extra height and quickly swiped the dust gathered there.

"I'm finished now." Her voice was husky, his touch having the effect it had always had.

"What are you doing here?" she questioned querulously as he set her back on the floor, his hand curving around her ass before patting it affectionately.

"I wanted to see you before heading to the house. Since you're going to be so busy, I thought I'd stop off here before putting in some extra hours getting things together. It should be ready soon."

Ready for what?

"That's good." She cleared her throat as she moved back from him even as she let her eyes eat him up. Damn, he looked good. Too good.

His blond hair was short, but finally starting to grow out of the shorter, GQ cut he had adopted for some reason. Freshly shaven, dressed in boots and jeans and a crisp blue shirt that brought out the gray in his eyes.

"Yeah, real good," he growled. "It'll be nice to finally be home." He crossed his arms over his chest, almost glaring back at her. "I want you to move in with me."

She blinked at him in surprise.

"Really?" She met his stance, jutting her hip out, placing her hand casually upon it as she stared at him implacably. "Isn't that too bad. I have a home, Slade, and I like it fine."

"You don't need it full-time anymore, Jessie," he argued firmly, obviously determined to win. "I have a nice big bed and plenty of room. You can fix it up just the way you like it. However you want it." She could hear the wheedling offer. And it was tempting, damned tempting.

"I like things just the way I have them at the apartment." She shook her head in determination. She wasn't ready for this, to give him that much of herself. Not yet.

He frowned. A completely male look of frustration and manipulation glittering in his eyes.

"I don't like leaving you at night," he growled. "I want you in my bed with me, Jessie."

"And you're a big boy, Slade," she crooned, her smile sweetly mocking. "I promise the bogeyman won't get you."

"He might get you if you don't stop being so damned stubborn," he grunted. "I'm not going to leave you again, Jessie. I swear—"

"And I'm not a toy you can throw down then come back and pick up whenever you get an urge to. Life doesn't work like that, Slade. I don't care how many assurances you give me, I'm not moving in with you." She almost laughed at the narrow-eyed determination that filled his expression.

"I'll put the house in your name." Sheer male arrogance filled his face then. "We'll do the paperwork this week—"

"Slade, it's not going to happen. I don't want your house, I'm not going to be your little playmate, and I'm not moving in with you. Forget it. We're not married, stud. I have a choice here."

"Then marry me," he snapped. "It's not like we're not headed that way anyway."

Sheer shock ricocheted through her.

"My, aren't we romantic today?" She shook her head, the sarcasm dripping from her as she watched him. "You just don't get it, do you, Slade? I'm not a kid anymore. I'm not a piece of clay you can shape and mold and make decisions for. I don't even know if I like you..."

"You love me. Why do you keep trying to hide it?"

She pressed her lips together tightly. "Says who?"

"Says that tight little ass you turned up for me last night," he growled, a spark of anger filling his eyes. "Deny it. Go ahead, Jessie, tell me Jazz had that part of you too? That you would ever trust someone you don't love so fully?"

"Maybe Jazz wasn't my only lover, Slade," she suggested archly. "What makes you think I filled my days with a man I didn't love and that I knew would never love me? I could have had dozens of lovers."

"You and Jazz and your goddamned fucking maybes," he snarled. "You didn't do shit, baby girl. You waited on me." His arms jerked from his chest, his thumb pointing back to his heart. "You know it and I know it, and by God, I don't see any sense in playing games now."

"Like the games you played five years ago?" She wasn't going to get angry, she promised herself. Slade wasn't going to steamroll over her and it was that simple. He wanted back in her life, fine, he could play it her way or he could find another game to play. "Come on, Slade, tell me why you ran off and married Amy Jennings? Better yet, why come back now, five years later, and only after her death?"

"You're pissing me off, Jessie," he bit out. "I told you, we'll discuss all this soon..."

"And I don't care if we ever discuss it," she flung back at him, moving to gather a load of books to place on the shelves as though the discussion had nothing to do with her heart, her soul. "You left with another woman. You stayed gone. No phone call, no letters, no emails. Nothing but a nice little goodbye and a reminder of what a child I was," she reminded him casually, keeping the remembered pain from her voice as she couldn't keep it from her heart.

Jessie shoved the books onto a lower shelf, breathing in deeply as she felt him behind her, watching her. Since she was sixteen, barely aware of what she was inviting when she set her heart on him. She had felt his gaze the first time he realized she was becoming a woman. The surprise, the heat. She had been aware of him from that moment forward, as though some mystic bond tied them together, refusing to let them free.

"There was more to it." The words seemed forced from him. "Things you don't know—"

"Things I don't care to know." She was lying. She was dying to know. It was a fever in her blood she couldn't rid herself of. But damn him, he had left her. She would never, ever give him that kind of power over her again.

She slammed another stack of books onto the shelf as he stayed silent behind her.

"Why do you do this?" She turned on him, frustrated, irritated, not just by him but by her response to him. "I didn't ask you to come back here. I didn't ask you to mess with my damned head again."

"Didn't you?" he snarled back at her. "You tortured me every night I managed to sleep; filling my dreams, tormenting me with the remembered feel of your heat and your hunger." He stalked toward her, pressing her into the shelf before jerking her into his arms. "You're fighting a fine fight, baby, trying to convince yourself and me that you don't love, that you don't give a fuck." His lips drew back from his teeth in a feral smile. "I know better. I know, because I feel it every time I touch you, every time I take you. So don't bother to fucking lie to me."

"Like you lied to me?" she finally threw in his face. "What, Slade, do you have the corner on the liar's market?"

He released her slowly, his expression brooding, angry.

"Like I lied to you," he finally whispered. "And paid for it every single second of the past five years, Jessie. We both paid for it. I don't know about you, but I'm tired of the punishment. Get your pretty ass ready and you might as well settle yourself to it. Because you are mine." His finger pointed imperiously toward her chest. "And you will stay mine."

She opened her lips to blast him, to tell him exactly where he could shove his demands, his beliefs, his damned arrogance. A sharp knock on the closed door had them springing apart instead.

"Damn you," she muttered, striding quickly to the door and pushing it open slowly.

Clarissa Jennings stood on the other side of the door, her pinched expression reminding Jessie of the fact that the other woman was just as vindictive as her first cousin had been. As part of the faculty, Jessie had no choice but to put up with the principal from hell. Her first year teaching last year had been so hard due to this woman's ineptitude that Jessie had requested a transfer at the end of the year. It hadn't come through yet.

"I need to talk to Slade. I saw him come in earlier and assume he's here." Disapproval and distaste marked her angular features.

"Oh, Slade." Jessie turned, smiling at him sweetly. "You're being paged."

What she saw on Slade's face was frightening. The look he gave Clarissa was filled with fury, with warning. Just enough to cause the other woman to step back as Jessie stared between them in confusion.

"I was just leaving," he growled, stopping before Jessie as he stared at her in reminder. "I'll see you later."

"Only if I don't see you coming first," she muttered.

He grunted, reaching out to snag her hair as he pulled her head back for a quick, hard kiss, ignoring Clarissa's sniff of disdain.

"Later, baby." He smiled tightly before turning from her, his fingers gripping Clarissa's arm and steering her quickly up the hall.

Okay. Now she wanted the answers. And she was going to get them soon.

* * *

Slade slammed the door to his jeep, stalking up the front steps to the Jennings home with an edge of fury. Clarissa was a bitch, nearly as fucking vindictive as her cousin had been. He banged on the front door, hearing

Cody's cries of glee as he glimpsed him through the door window.

The door opened quickly and the little boy threw himself into his father's arms.

Sturdy, but so damned reed-thin Slade worried that the boy was starving despite the amount of food he ate. Hair as dark as a walnut and eyes a stunning turquoise. Cody had taught Slade the meaning of true innocence. The child had kept him going through some of the bleakest days of his life.

"Grammy said you wasn't going to come back," Cody cried as he buried his face against Slade's chest. "That I couldn't live in the big house with you like you said we were. Why is she lying to me, Daddy?" He gazed up at Slade fiercely. "I like the big house."

Anger tore through him. Just as his mother had, his grandmother was now trying to use the hold this child had on him to control him. Amy had gotten away with it simply because she could. He'd be damned if he'd let her parents.

"Not to worry, little buddy." He patted his son's back, glaring at Glenda and Hank Jennings as they moved into the hall. "We're moving in real soon. You and me both." And, he prayed, Jessie.

Sitting Cody down, he pointed him to the sandbox in the front yard. "You go play, let Daddy talk to Grammy and Gran'pa. Okay?"

He brushed the hair from Cody's forehead, marveling at the innocence in the boy's turquoise eyes.

Cody glared at his grandparents before turning back and hitching his jeans up on his little hips. "I'll play, but you tell 'em, Daddy. I get to live with you in the big house and that's that."

"That's that, little man." Slade nodded firmly. "You go play, I'll take care of it."

He stared at the older couple as Cody ran out to the sand pile.

"Hank." Slade turned to the older man, deferring to the man's normally placid temperament. "You want to tell me why Clarissa thinks she can tell me who you will allow around my son and who you think you won't?"

Clarissa's demand had been concise as she cornered him in the Principal's office of the school. He would not, in any way, see Jessie again or Cody's grandparents would sue for custody of the child.

When he left the office, Clarissa had been pale, shaking, utterly convinced that she had stared death in the face and barely escaped when he left. He hoped it kept her mouth shut just a little bit longer.

Now, he just had to deal with Glenna and Hank.

"That woman destroyed Amy, Slade," Glenna accused, tears filling her voice. "Do you think she didn't tell us how miserable you made her because of that little slut?"

"Enough!" It was a damned good thing Glenna said it and not Hank. He wouldn't hit a woman, but Amy had gotten her vindictive mouth from somewhere. He turned to Hank. "I can take Cody now and not come back, Hank. I won't have this. That boy is innocent and I won't have his head messed with. I was faithful to Amy and treated her like gold. You know I did. She's gone now, and I'll be damned if Cody will pay for the problems we had."

"You didn't love her." Hank shook his head wearily, his eyes sad. "She was in that car because of you."

"She was in that car because that was where she wanted to be," he growled, wishing he could tell them the truth, wishing the Top Secret stamp on her file didn't forbid him from revealing the information. "If she wanted that marriage to work she would have tried, the same as I was. It wasn't Jessie's fault, it wasn't Cody's. And neither of them are going to be punished because of it."

He was furious and thanked God, not for the first time, that they were unaware of the fact that Cody wasn't his biological child. They would have taken him in a heartbeat.

"I'm taking him with me now," he snapped, battling the wild anger growing inside him as he speared Hank with a remorseless look. "You two better think this over and decide how important it is to you to continue this vendetta. If it keeps up, I'll make sure you never see Cody again."

He didn't give them a chance to argue. He turned, stomping back to the yard and swinging his son into his arms.

"What say we start work on the house early today?" He hoisted the boy to his shoulders as he moved to the jeep. "We could go ahead and put up the fence around the yard. That sound good?"

Cody threw out a *yee haw* that had Slade laughing in delight, and his heart lightened. He deposited Cody in the back toddler seat, strapped him in and moved around the front of the vehicle.

As he jumped into his seat and snapped his seat belt, he threw another hard look back to the couple standing on the porch, and felt his chest tighten with heaviness. He hoped to stay on friendly terms with Amy's parents. Cody needed his family, grandparents. He didn't have aunts or uncles, but he could have had the extended family the Jennings possessed if they would pull the sticks out of their asses long enough to see the truth.

Not for the first time he thanked God that Jessie lived nowhere near Amy's family. The neighboring county wasn't one she associated with much. It was one Slade hadn't associated with much, until Amy. But it served as a reminder that he was going to have to tell her about Cody and the reason he had left her five years ago. Soon. If he didn't, someone else would.

Chapter Seventeen

The next morning, before the fog had even lifted from the ground, Slade pulled into the offices of Rigor Construction and parked his jeep beside Jessie's car. The small lake next to the offices kept the fog heavy, and lent the two-story office building a charm it wouldn't have had otherwise.

The small dock that led from the steep bank held Jazz's fishing boat and Zack's Sea-Doo. Their toys, which they played with often. Slade shook his head, but admitted the evenings they had spent fishing on the water were some of his best memories, besides that weekend he had spent with Jessie. Which brought him full circle. The situation with Amy's parents was getting out of hand.

He had dropped Cody off at his grandparents for the last time, he feared. Glenna had been openly hostile toward Slade, though she had gentled momentarily with Cody. Hank had been silent, his head hanging dejectedly in the face of his wife's anger. It was something Cody didn't need to be a part of, and to be honest, Slade was growing sick of the woman's waspishness. It wasn't a healthy atmosphere for his child. Today, he had two objectives. Find someone else to watch the boy, and this evening, tell Jessie the truth.

First, he needed one more taste of her. God, he missed her last night. The woman was under his skin like a fever. She always had been, and he had admitted, even before leaving her, that nothing was going to cure him of it.

He stepped up to her apartment door, his lips quirked at the note taped on it.

If this note is here, I'm still sleeping. Go away until a decent hour.

He snorted, inserted the key into the lock and turned it with a silent click. The door slid open, enclosing him in a rush of warm air. Damn, it was too warm in here. Despite the open windows and the early morning air, it was thick with sultry heat.

He stepped through the interior, moving into the bedroom as he pulled his shirt off. Sitting on the padded chest against the wall he removed his boots, staring at the woman sleeping on the bed, sprawled naked beneath a light blanket. Her hair fanned out around her flushed face, her lips parted with seductive sensuality as she breathed deeply.

Shucking his jeans and shorts, he pulled at the blanket, drawing it slowly from her lithe, lovely body, smiling as she muttered in her sleep. A frown creased her brow as his cock jerked in lusty demand. A smile tugged at his lips as he bared her breasts, the flushed mounds with their delicate pink, hardened nipples. The air in the bedroom grew warmer.

The material slid down her torso, her abdomen, revealing the little tattoo, the dragon he so loved. God, he dreamed of kissing her there again, of feeling the heat of her flesh, smelling the scent of her arousal from the soft folds below. Then the blanket cleared her thighs, revealing her bare pussy. Damn, the sight of that tattoo never failed to weaken him. It was just so Jessie. Whimsical, reminding him of fairy tales and the love he had so feared he had lost.

She was his light. The very air he breathed and he had no clue how to convince her of this, how to convince her that the past would never be repeated, that he had known, even before he left her, exactly what he was walking away from.

With the blanket now lying on the floor and Jessie's soft body revealed to him, thoughts of anything but loving her, touching her, fled his mind. Just looking at her seduced his senses, filled him with visions of her writhing beneath him, as consumed as he was with their passion. It also filled him with tenderness. The mix of emotions kept him off balance, reminding him often of the power this one little woman held over him.

His chest tight with emotions that often seemed too intense, Slade lowered himself beside her, feeling her turn instantly to him, snuggling against his chest with a sleepy little sigh. He hated the thought of awakening her just yet, despite the need pounding through his body. He was rarely given the chance to just hold her as she slept, curled trustingly to his heart as her legs tangled with his. His fingers threaded through her hair, the feel of cool silk against his palm reminding him of untold nights when he had lain alone, staring into the darkness, his soul filled with memories of her. The need to touch her had been overwhelming, his knowledge that only the distance between them had saved his own sense of honor had been a bitter pill to swallow.

If he hadn't left her, he would have never made the choices he had made, because God knew she was like a fever in his blood that he had no desire to be rid of.

"Told you I was sleeping," she muttered against his chest, her body still relaxed, curving trustingly against him. "I knew you would show up at a miserable hour."

Smiling, he brushed her hair back from her cheek, his hand cupping the side of her face as he laid a kiss against the corner of her mouth.

"I missed you," he whispered, keeping his voice hushed, determined to hold onto the edge of fantasy that wrapped around them.

She stretched against him, silken legs rubbing against his rougher ones as she curled closer, his arms tightening around her.

"We have to talk today, Slade," she finally sighed, her hands pressing against his hair-roughened chest, her lips caressing his neck.

Slade closed his eyes. Yeah, they had to talk today. But not right now. Not when the early morning fog enfolded them and she was lying sweet and relaxed against him.

"I love you, Jessie." He had to whisper the words, to reinforce the emotion that had backed his decisions for the past five years.

"But sometimes love isn't enough." The saddened remembrances in her voice pricked at the comfort enfolding.

"And sometimes, love is all you have." For five years he had lived on the memory of love. He couldn't survive on the memory any longer. "We'll talk tonight. There's a lot I have to tell you and decisions we both have to make. But I don't want to talk right now. Right now, I just want your love."

She tilted her head back, her velvety brown eyes drowsy.

"You always had my love, Slade. Every minute of every day for as long as I've known you. But I'm not a child anymore. And I don't need your protection." Her voice was laced with steel, her gaze becoming direct, determined.

"I'll protect you with my life whenever it's necessary, Jessie." He sighed. Hell, he didn't know anything else. "You're my sunlight. I've been without you too long, I've needed you too much. That is never going to change."

"Then we're going to have a hell of a time figuring this relationship out," she warned him, the drowsy sensuality that filled her face doing nothing to detract from the defiance in her eyes. "You might be the big bad stud, but I'll be damned if you'll roll me as though the past never happened and it can be wiped away by the simple means of never speaking of it. It doesn't work that way for me. It won't work that way for me."

"I know, baby." And that weighed heaviest on his heart. He wanted to forget. He wanted to close the door on the pain behind them and never open it again. "Just let me hold you right now, while the morning is quiet around us, while you're soft and sweet from sleep and just mine. Let me have that for now."

"You always had that." Her hand lifted, her fingers brushing over his jaw before feathering over his lips. "But it's not free this time, Slade. This time, I want all of you. The secrets you're holding and the reasons you left. Everything. Or you can walk out that door now and never come back."

"Never," he growled, the fierce denial tearing through his chest as he pulled her harder against him. "Believe that, Jessie. No matter what you think, no matter how much you may dislike the decisions I've made or will make, I'll never walk away again. Ever."

"I will." Regret shimmered in her eyes. "I won't be lied to, Slade. And I won't be played with. Never again."

He pushed her to her back, knowing the culmination of five years was rapidly closing in on him and the fear that tightened his chest sickened him, terrified him.

"I'll drag you back," he warned her. "And if I have to do that I'll tie you to my bed and I'll hold you there until you can't fight anymore, Jessie. I warned you years ago you didn't know what you were getting into, and I'm warning you now. I will not tolerate ever fucking losing you again."

Stretching her arms above her head he held them there as he stole her protests by the simple means of silencing them with his kiss. It wasn't a ravaging, greedy kiss, though God knew he was desperate to taste her. He used the caress to disarm her instead. Slanting his lips over hers, he sipped at her, tasted her. His tongue stroked past the parted curves, retreating just as quickly, relishing the sound of her broken breaths as he threw himself into the fire that was so much a part of her.

Her breasts pressed against his chest, hot little nipples searing his flesh, but nothing was as good as her kiss. He tugged at her lips with his own, licked at them, tasted her, dipped into her mouth and let her flow around him. His heart was reborn in her. Five years of deprivation and aching loneliness. It would take a lifetime to still the hunger now. It would take forever to ease it. He would never forget, never let himself relax in the vigilance that he never, ever lose her again.

"Warm me, Jessie," he whispered against her lips, his teeth tugging at the lower curve, his desperation to hold onto her transferring to his refusal to release her lips. She stared back at him, passion and anger warring in her gaze. "I've been so cold, baby. Bone-deep cold, where no fire can reach, only you. Don't let me be cold again."

Surrender echoed in her moan, in the flutter of her lashes as he rimmed her lips with his tongue. Sleep-soft, heated and filling the dark places in his soul, she relaxed beneath him, her little tongue peeking out, tempting him to burn in the center of the fire that was Jessie.

He touched her like the dream she had been for five long years. He released her hands, allowing his fingers to mold the firm curves of her breasts, as his lips moved down the smooth arch of her throat, heading unerringly to the baby pink, hard little nipples below.

She arched and cried out as he lashed at them with his tongue. Her fingers buried in his hair, her breath rasping as he suckled them into his mouth, raked over them with his teeth.

"So good..." Her whispering moan only fueled his lusts. "Better than the dreams, Slade. It's better than the dreams."

He groaned at the husky declaration. Yes, it was better than the dreams, hotter, deeper and he wanted more. He moved down her body, spreading her thighs wide as his head lowered and he kissed the wet folds of her pussy. He laid his lips against them, parted them with his tongue, licked through the narrow little slit and became intoxicated on her heat and her taste.

She was nectar. A fire in the winter. Summer's heat all winter long, and she filled him. Filled all the dark corners of his soul and gave him joy. This was joy. Holding her hips arched to his lips, fucking her with his tongue, licking at the weeping fall of her juices and hearing her ragged moans as they echoed around him.

As she unraveled in orgasm, he felt his chest expand in pride and possessiveness. She was his. Rising above her, he moved between her spread thighs, watching as his cock nudged against the flushed curves, his teeth gritting as he remembered the condom still tucked in his pants.

"Are you protected, baby?"

She stared at him, dark eyes filled with heat and hunger.

"I was never unprotected," she breathed out roughly.

He stared down at her, reliving Amy's announcement of her pregnancy, his horror, his terror that the weekend he had spent filling Jessie with his seed would destroy her life as well.

He glanced at her abdomen, a surge of emotion ripping through him at the thought of filling her with their child. Of seeing her sweet curves ripen, her belly heavy with a babe.

He licked his lips at the hunger.

"I want to have babies with you," he whispered, pressing inside her. "Soon. I want our child filling you. I want to tie you to me until there's no way in hell you can get away from me."

Her breathing hitched as he pulled his gaze back to her face and he saw the hunger there. Not just the hunger for the lust, for the release. The hungry dreams, the need to tie him to her as effectively as he would tie her to him.

He slid inside her, working his hips slowly, stroking each agonized inch of his cock into the fist-tight portal sucking him in. She rippled around him, clenched, convulsed, bound his soul with her touch, with her love.

"You would make beautiful babies, Jessie," he groaned, his voice rough as he seated himself inside her to the hilt. "Our babies."

"You're killing me, Slade," she whimpered, her eyes nearly black with emotion as she lifted to him, taking all of him with a pained little cry of pleasure. "Don't dream with me then take it all again."

The aching fear in her voice as her hands gripped his arms broke his heart all over again.

"Never again," he snarled, retreating, thrusting powerfully inside her. "I'll never lose you again, Jessie."

His hands dug into her hips as he began to move, the ability to speak, to think, disappearing rapidly beneath the passion consuming them both. He pounded inside her, feeling her pussy grip him, ripple around him, spasming and convulsing as she cried out hoarsely, finding her first release.

It wasn't enough. Not yet.

"Again." He growled, coming over her, lifting her legs and sinking deeper inside her.

She was wet, so silky-sweet and syrupy-slick that he growled in animalistic hunger against her throat. He couldn't get enough of her. Couldn't get deep enough, hard enough. And she was so fucking tight that each stroke was like pushing inside a velvet vise that tightened and wrung every ounce of pleasure from his soul.

"Hold me, Jessie." Her arms were tight around his shoulders, but he wasn't close enough. The heat of her seared him, washing over him, through him, warming him. But he had to get closer, had to mark her, bind her to him forever.

Her arms tightened around him, her body quickened beneath him, but the words he needed didn't fall from her lips. Didn't echo in the air around them, and he knew it wasn't something he could force from her.

She had given him her love unconditionally once before, and now he was fighting for it. Begging for it.

He moved harder, deeper, snarling with the pleasure and the pain of loving her, taking her. Her cries shattered the stillness of the air as he lunged desperately inside her over and over again. He fucked her with a desperation that would have shocked him had he the sense to pay attention. All he knew was the pleasure, the incredible hunger and the love ripping through him.

As she exploded beneath him again, her pussy rippling and clenching around him, reality darkened. His only pinpoint of light was Jessie as he felt the sizzling warning of his release race up his spine and fill his head.

He thrust harder, his hips pounding against her, his cock stroking furiously inside the melting heat of her pussy until he came apart as well. Driving deeper, fighting to become a part of her forever, he felt his release shatter him. Hard, blinding, his semen shot from his dick, filling her, flooding her with rich, heated seed, searching for that ultimate bond, the dream that had filled him for years.

Jessie.

Chapter Eighteen

"We have a date this evening," Slade reminded her as she lay in drowsy, sated splendor on the bed after another bout of mind-blowing sex. The man was a walking orgasm. A bone-melting, rocking, incredible orgasm waiting to happen. Her pussy still throbbed from the pounding he had given it, even as it ached with satisfied pleasure.

"We don't have a date." She stretched, laziness filling her as her eyes drifted closed and a nice long nap became a major consideration.

The silence that followed her statement wasn't noticeable to her at first. Her senses were still dazed, her nervous system on overload. There was nothing quite like sex with Slade. It did something to her. Made her drunk or high or maybe sedated? It was better than any drug she had ever heard of. And she guessed, working as she did with some of the more precocious kids at the school, she had heard of most of the current drugs.

Maybe it was adrenaline overload, she thought lazily. Didn't you fall really fast when you crashed from it?

"Jessie, I'll be back tonight..."

"...don't wanna hear it." She really didn't. It was like tempting fate. She had been there before, she didn't like it then and she was going to like it even less as a second dose of disillusionment.

She heard his sigh and ignored that too. She was just too damned boneless to argue right now. Of course, if he wanted to lie down beside her, maybe nap just a little bit before he rushed off to that stupid meeting, she could handle that. They hadn't talked much, she realized. From the moment he had burst his way back into her life, they hadn't done much but fuck. It was a helluva way to spend a summer day, but she had to admit, she was beginning to wish for more. Beginning to crave more.

She wanted to spend the night in his arms. Wanted to share dreams, and tell him about the kids at school, the bitch principal from hell. She wanted to hear about his day at work, listen to his dry humor as he recounted his day to her. She wanted more than just the sex and that had the power to piss her off.

As she lay there, she could have sworn she felt a breath of air at her hip, a light caress on the tattoo placed there. A fragile memory flitted through her mind. Midnight, a party raging outside as she slipped into sleep, the feel of Slade's eyes watching her, his lips at her hip, seconds later his voice at her ear.

Take my heart with you, baby girl. It follows you...always... The sound of his pain, his voice hoarse, ragged, as torn as her soul. As though it had actually happened, rather than a wishful dream, a kernel of hope to keep her heart warm. She was pathetic, she admitted, not for the first time. A walking, talking fool for one man.

She opened her eyes, staring down where he knelt beside the bed, his head raising from her hip. Chills raced up her spine as he stared back at her, his gaze still holding the shadows of a bleak, grief-torn pain.

The words were on the tip of her lips, knowledge fighting to find its way through as she pushed it ruthlessly back. She wouldn't revisit the past, she swore to herself. She was taking one day at a time with him, one touch at a time. If and when he was gone again, she would survive, knowing she had expected nothing more.

A resigned quirk tugged at his lips. "I'll never leave you again, Jessie."

She shook her head, that clenching cold chill racing over her scalp as that memory whispered through her head again.

"No promises, Slade." She reached up, her fingers brushing over his beard-stubbled jaw as he caught her hand, holding it to his cheek. "I have to survive. No promises."

He shook his head, weariness filling his expression before he clenched his teeth in irritation. Irritation on Slade's face amused her. He had a way of lowering his brows, slicing into you with those stormy eyes, and making most people wish they had never crossed paths with him to begin with. It had always made her laugh.

"I'll be back tonight." He laid his fingers across her lips as she began to negate the statement. "Tonight, Jessie. Bet on it."

She wasn't a betting woman. Not anymore.

He rose, giving her one last, brooding look.

"You've carried my heart, all this time. Hell, you owned my soul. Don't ask me to stop dreaming of you, or to stop asking for tomorrow. Because for five fucking years the hope that came with each tomorrow was all I fucking had left. Remember that."

He turned and stomped from the bedroom then the apartment as Jessie frowned up at the ceiling.

Take my heart with you, baby girl. It follows you...always...

Shaking away the chill of premonition, she rose from the bed. Forget sleep, she would only dream. Lately, her dreams had been too shadowed, too disturbing to want to face again. The only time she didn't dream of him was when he held her. The nights were long, restless, her need to feel his warmth against her overwhelming.

She should have demanded answers by now, she thought as she dragged herself to the shower and scrubbed at her body angrily. She should have demanded answers before she ever allowed him to touch her. But she hadn't. Too stupid to live, she thought with a sigh as she dried and pulled on her bathing suit and wrap. The clear water of the small lake outside the office building pulled at her. Her float was secured in the seat of Jazz's fishing boat, and the sun was coming up hot and bright. She was going to enjoy it before lesson plans, parent-teacher meetings, and the stress of the school year began. She hadn't time to worry about Slade or his reasons for anything. She told herself there was no excuse for his actions five years before. If he had loved her, truly loved her, they could have worked through anything.

Stepping from the building, she let a smile tug at her lips as she heard the ducks quacking at the end of the dock. There were dozens of small groups of the cute little fiends that fought for every scrap of food they could find. As she walked across the parking lot, shock soared within her as she saw the small scrap of humanity squatting at the edge of the floating walkway, leaning forward, hands outstretched for one precious feathered baby.

"Oh my God. Oh my God." She began to race along the path, knowing she would never get there in time. Never... "Oh my God. Slade! Jazz. Help me!" She was screaming as the baby toppled into the water, his little head disappearing into the murky depths as she tore her wrap from her shoulders and dived in.

The warm water enclosed her, deep, too fucking deep. And dark. The child's hair was dark as well, and vision was severely limited beneath the dark waters.

She stretched, kicking her feet, her hands moving frantically before her as she fought to feel for the child's dark head. He couldn't have sunk far, she thought irrationally. He couldn't weigh enough. He was such a little scrap he couldn't have gone far. But the fall to the water was nearly four feet, it would have given him enough momentum with the way his body had curled, reaching for that damned duck.

Where are you? she screamed silently, staring through the murky depths desperately. *Oh God. Let me find him. Let me find him.*

Fighting to push deeper, searching desperately, she could feel the pressure in her chest growing tighter, the need for oxygen consuming her when she caught the faintest glimmer of pale flesh. Reaching out mindlessly, her fingers finally tangled in soft silky hair and pulled as she began kicking for the surface. Securing the child in her arms, she struggled now to save them both. Hard hands grabbed her waist and propelled her through the life-taking depths, causing her to burst to the surface faster than she could have herself.

She broke through the water, gulping in air, the lax little body in her arms terrifying her as she saw Jazz's pale face reaching for the body. She lifted the boy to him as Slade scrambled to the floating deck, an enraged howl tearing from his throat.

"Cody!" His resounding cry had her turning shocked eyes to where Jazz and Zack were working to expel the water from the baby's lungs, begging him to breathe.

"Oh God! Cody. Baby! Breathe for Daddy, Cody. Breathe." Slade bent, blew into the mouth and nostrils, rising as Jazz massaged the tiny chest and Zack checked the pulse in the skinny little arm.

Slade's face was wet and not just from the plunge he had taken into the water after her. Tears rained from his eyes, filled his voice as he prayed.

As though in slow motion, Jessie watched, her heart bursting in her chest as sobs fought to tear free.

"Oh God! Cody, please..." Slade bent, breathing into the child's mouth again as Jazz and Zack cursed, screamed.

Suddenly, the little body jerked, convulsed and water streamed from his nose and mouth. A whimpering cry turned into a terror-filled wail for his daddy as Slade jerked him into his arms. Rocking him, his arms surrounded the child as he buried his face in his wet hair.

Slade's face was white, his body shuddering. Not that she blamed him, the child was a stranger to her and she was shaking, shock and confusion ripping through her mind. She couldn't believe it. She told herself there was no way she could have suspected it. And yet, the proof was there.

"Daddy has you, Son." He rubbed at the little boy's fragile back, his big hands appearing large against such a tiny body. "It's okay, Son. Daddy has you."

"Jessie." Jazz knelt beside her, pushing back at her hair as she stared at Slade and his child. "Are you okay, Jessie? Your cheek is bleeding."

She reached up, touched her cheek absently. She barely remembered the duck that had been unfortunate enough to be in her way as she dove in after the little boy. But it didn't hurt. Nothing could hurt enough to still the pain raging in her soul.

Slade's child.

He was rocking the baby, a tiny scrap of skinny arms and legs that gasped and gripped at the broad shoulders of the man holding him. His daddy.

He whimpered, "Daddy...I just wanted the duckie..." He coughed, strangling on water before his air pipes cleared again. "The duckie, Daddy..." Sobs were muted, the terror fading as his daddy rocked him, clutched him to him, whispering senseless, comforting "daddy" things into his ear.

"Jessie?" Jazz turned her face to him, his deep blue eyes compassionate. "Are you okay, sweet pea?"

She rose shakily to her feet, stumbling away from him, pushing at his hands as he tried to right her.

Slade's child, and he hadn't told her. He hadn't told her when he ran away with Amy, leaving Jessie to grieve, to ache, to pray for a miracle and a child that would ease her pain. He had given that child to Amy instead.

"Jessie." Jazz's voice was soft, brimming with understanding. "Come here, girl. Let me make sure you're okay."

Let him hold her there until Slade could breathe, could realize what had happened. Let him do as he had done in another fashion, save her for Slade. She shook her head, slapping at his hands as she moved away from him. She jerked her wrap from the deck, pulling it on, feeling the keys that rattled in the pocket.

She held her hand out in denial to Jazz as he reached for her again.

"No." Her voice was raspy, the tears she held inside smothering her as she moved quickly past them all. "Just...no."

She had to get away. She had to escape Slade and his buddies, the men who watched out for each other, no matter what. What was the pact? Jazz had told her once. The Three Musketeers thing? She couldn't remember, but as she raced for her car she didn't care.

He hadn't told her. He had left, letting her believe he loved another woman, that she wasn't mature enough, wasn't woman enough to hold him. And he had returned, hiding the truth from her, hiding the child from her. Why? Because he didn't trust her. Because he still saw her as that useless, immature child he obviously thought she was. A good fuck, but not good enough to trust. Not good enough to have his baby, despite his proclamation before.

She jabbed the key into the lock, her hands shaking so hard now it was all she could do to unlock the door. The interior was stifling, almost as smothering as the agony twisted inside her.

The sobs tore from her chest as she locked the door behind her, letting the heated recesses of the vehicle enclose her. She couldn't... Sob's ripped through as her vision became cloudy with her tears. What had she done?

Chapter Nineteen

Too stupid to live.

Jessie drove the car without a thought to where she was heading, her heart and her mind a morass of emotions, a shattered cauldron of the past and the present, dreams both broken and barely formed. She couldn't erase the memory from her mind of Slade's face as he held that child. Stark white, his eyes so dark they looked smoke-black, tears filling them, the whites bloodshot from the water and his horror.

His two hands had covered the child's back, it was so small. His chest heaving, strangled breaths filled with tears tearing from his chest as he continued to run his hands over his child's body, assuring himself he was okay. That no bones were broken. That he was breathing. That he was indeed safe. He was indeed alive.

The love she had glimpsed in Slade's face had been like a bolt of lightning ripping through her mind, ripping away the excuses she consoled herself with, and making her admit to her own failures, her own immaturity.

"It's okay, baby, Daddy has you. Daddy will take care of you...Daddy's got you, baby..."

Daddy. The love Slade felt for that child was clear in his voice, on his face. It twisted his expression into lines of horror and rage as he fought to force the water from the small lungs, begging God, praying for his life.

She didn't know what to do. Where to go. What to think or to feel.

She couldn't go to Jazz. The boys' club was intact, she had learned that the moment she realized Slade had returned. The son of a bitch had given her to Jazz, left another man to watch over her, to *protect* her as though she were a witless child.

Jazz and Zack were out of the question. Where did that leave her?

Her sisters lived states away and her mother was sunning on the beach in Florida. Where *she* should be, Jessie thought. She could be lying on the beach, soaking up the rays with no little men's club in sight. She could have had lovers, real lovers. Men who wanted her because she deserved to be wanted, not because they were a pseudo stand-in determined to save her nonexistent virtue for the bastard who left her for another woman.

No, not another woman. She knew better. Now.

He had left her for the child. Amy must have been pregnant when he married her, there was no other explanation. Slade would have never left a child of his to be raised by others, no matter what he had to give up for it. He would have sacrificed anything for that baby. And Jessie knew Amy. The other woman had been calculating, manipulative. A true bitch with a mean streak a mile long.

Hell, she was just like her cousin, Clarissa, the principal from hell.

Another woman had borne the child Jessie had prayed for. It ripped through her, ripped inside her. The baby she had prayed to be carrying five years before, and Amy had borne it instead.

She wiped at the tears falling down her face, hating herself for crying, for hurting. For being so damned shocked. He *had* loved her. She had known then, just as she knew now. She hadn't been wrong about the emotion she had seen in Slade's eyes, in his face. Not then and not now. It was the reason she had given into him so easily when he returned to claim her. It was also the reason she had fought asking him why. Why had he left her? Why hadn't he explained how he could have loved her and walked away? Because she had known only one thing would force Slade to make such a decision.

He had been raised without a family, without security. Shuttled from one foster home to another nearly all his life, Slade had never known permanence, he had never known security. Zack had told her once that Slade had sworn he would never allow a child of his to live such a life. That he would not let his baby go without his name, or his protection. She had pushed aside the obvious message in what he was saying. She had ignored the lifeline he had thrown to her soul.

Just as she had ignored what her soul had tried to tell her from that first night. Slade wasn't like most men. His own personal desires or hungers would never dictate to his sense of responsibility or what he knew was right or wrong.

Take my heart with you, baby girl. It follows you...always...

It hadn't been a dream. That night in Jazz's RV, she had been certain she was dreaming that Slade touched her, that his voice had flowed around her, broken, filled with regret and love. She hadn't been dreaming, he had been there, his hands brushing back her hair, his lips caressing the tattoo, then the shell of her ear.

Take care of her, Jazz... His voice had been ragged when he whispered those words.

The scattered words that had made no sense for the past five years now fell into place. She hadn't been able to make sense of the dream because it hadn't been a dream. Just as she hadn't been able to understand why she hadn't tried to love anyone else. For years she had drifted in this little pocket, staying in the center of Slade's friends, feeding from the smallest bit of information she heard about him. Her heart leaping when she heard he was coming home, her soul rousing in joy when she saw him again the first time. And through it all, she had refused to understand why he had left.

She had been too immature. Her own pain, her own desperation to feel Slade's arms around her again had been all that mattered. She had convinced herself he hadn't loved her yet she had never been able let him go. She had let herself believe he loved another woman, that he chose a woman who would fit into the life he obviously wanted better than she would. She had let herself believe she had failed him with her youth. It hadn't been her youth that had failed him. It had been something much deeper, much more important. She had failed to believe in him, when she had known to the bottom of her soul that Slade would not have betrayed her without paying the cost himself.

What had she done?

She guided the vehicle onto the main road, her hands curled around the wheel with desperate fingers. Slade hadn't failed her.

She had failed Slade.

*   *   *

Slade cradled Cody close to his chest as he found the strength in his weakened legs to straighten and watch as Jessie headed away from the parking lot. He had seen her face, the hollow shock, the blinding pain that had sent her running from him. God, he just couldn't stop hurting her, could he?

"I'm sorry, Daddy." Cody sniffed against his chest, his thin little arms latched around his neck as he still shook in fear.

"Come on, little guy." Slade's voice was rough, raw from the enraged howl that had torn free of his throat when he saw who Jessie carried in her arms from the murky waters as he pulled her to the surface. "Let's get you dry."

He pressed Cody's head to his chest, moving quickly for the office building and Jazz's apartment on the main floor as Jazz and Zack flanked him. If it hadn't been for the opened deck doors they would have never heard Jessie's screams, or the hysterical terror in her voice. He could have lost his child and the woman he loved in the dark waters of that lake, and never known until it was too late.

"Cody, where's Gramma, baby?" He sat his son on the kitchen counter, pushing back the unruly dark brown hair as he gazed into the turquoise eyes still filled with tears and fear.

"Gramma said go here..." Cody whimpered. "To your office. I just wanted to pet the duckies first, Daddy." He gazed imploringly back at his daddy. "I couldn't breathe, Daddy." His eyes were still wild with terror.

Slade felt rage consume him. A blinding, overwhelming murderous rage as his head swung to Zack.

"I called the sheriff." Zack's arms were crossed over his chest. "This was criminal, Slade. Let them deal with her. Never let the crazy bitch around him again. But you won't go after her yourself."

Slade flattened his lips as Cody's sobs began to jerk his little body. God damn. He was just a baby. Too small for his age, all skinny arms and legs and big blue eyes. He was gasping for breath right now, on the edge of hyperventilation. Cody had suffered from it for years, his fears often throwing him into complete panic, even before Amy's death.

"Settle down, baby." Slade took the towel from Jazz, wrapping it around Cody's shivering body and rubbing his hands over him firmly. "It's okay, little man. No blood, no tears. Remember? Are you bleeding?"

The words nearly choked him, ripped his heart from his body and left it bleeding on the floor. He shouldn't have to encourage his son to be strong, to fight the inability to breathe, to push back his fears.

"No blood...Daddy..." Cody hiccupped wildly.

"Then you're okay, right? Nothing to be scared of, little man. It's all okay now."

Cody nodded fiercely against his chest, though it was still several moments before he could fight past the panic raging through his little body.

"That's a good boy," Slade crooned.

Cody's breathing began to even out, the lessons his father had taught him for the past years taking over automatically. He had fought to teach his son, even at an early age, to think. To use his head, not his fears. Doing that now sucked.

Cody stared up at him trustingly, his eyes still swimming with tears but the beginning stages of hyperventilation were slowly easing.

"Grammy left you here, Cody?" Slade fought to keep his voice gentle. "Where was Grampa?"

"We was gonna buy ice creams and chips." Cody's lower lip puckered out in a pout. "Grampa didn't want any. Gramma wanted to ask you something, but when you came out of the other door, she got really mad and wouldn't take me. She said you would take me, Daddy."

Glenna had seen him leaving Jessie's apartment. Her spite and unreasonable anger toward Jessie and Slade over Amy's death had nearly killed his son. Sweet God, if it hadn't been for Jessie, for her quick thinking, Cody would have died.

Slade was a breath away from murder and he knew it. He had never, ever physically hurt a woman in his life, but Glenna Jennings was close, so fucking close to feeling his fingers around her throat that he feared he would leave her dead before he released her.

"Come on, Cody boy. How about we get you all dried up. I think Daddy needs a drink." Jazz moved beside them slowly, holding his arms out for the boy as Slade fought back the fury building in his gut.

"Are you tirsty, Daddy?" The childish lisp was accompanied by innocent eyes slowly drying of tears.

"Yeah. Daddy's thirsty, little man." He let Jazz lift him from the counter.

"We'll have to wash those clothes, little soldier," Jazz boomed as he turned away, holding Cody high on his chest. "Good thing Uncle Jazz has friends with kids. We just might be able to find you some skivvies."

The forced cheerfulness of Jazz's voice drove home to Slade the fact that he wasn't shaking alone. As Cody disappeared down the short hallway, Slade turned to Zack, the panic still beating like a runaway drum through his veins.

"Fuck! Bite my ass! Son of a bitch! I think I just lost ten years off my life. I'm too fucking old to be losing years, Slade," Zack was muttering as Jazz disappeared into one of the bedrooms with Cody, their laughter following them back. Slade jerked a cabinet door open and dragged the whisky from the interior.

Seconds later, the liquor was flowing down his throat, searing his guts as he braced his hand on the counter and fought for breath. Zack jerked the bottle from his hand and tilted it up straight.

"Jessie." Slade swallowed tightly. "You have to go find her. She didn't look good, Zack. Go take care of her."

"Not for all the wheat in Kansas," Zack snarled, turning back to him as he glowered furiously. "I leave you here alone and you'll draw blood. Jessie's stronger than you give her credit for, Slade. Let her get her head on straight and she'll be back. She won't stay gone for long."

Slade swiped his hand over his hair before jerking the bottle from Zack and refilling his glass. He could still hear Cody, his voice slowly returning to normal as he laughed at something Jazz was saying. Slade blinked back the dampness in his eyes, breathing carefully through the constriction in his chest.

"God, this is a fucking mess." Slade ran his fingers through his wet hair, only then realizing he was dripping on Jazz's kitchen floor.

"I told you to tell her," Zack growled. "You can't hide shit like this, Slade, it just bites you in the ass when you least expect it. She's not a fucking toy you can play with. She's been played with too much since you decided to pull that stupid-ass stunt five years ago and sneak away to the cove with her. We saved her for you. But you fuck it up now and all bets are off."

Slade stared back at him in surprise. "Jazz didn't save shit."

Zack grunted. "She was hurting, Slade. Bad. It was one of us or some other bumbling fool. You don't put a woman like that in fucking deep freeze. I'm too much like you. She didn't need rebound love, she needed a friend who could let her dream of you while he held her. Jazz was able to do that. I'm just too big of a prick for something like that, to be honest. If I were between her thighs, I'd be damned if I'd let her think about a danged fool like you." His midnight-blue eyes snapped with anger.

Slade had managed to avoid this conversation since returning. Now, he didn't give a damn. He could fight Zack just as easy as he could kill Glenna.

"I didn't expect her to wait," he bit out. "But I'd be damned if one of those bastards sniffing around her on a continual basis were good enough for her. All I asked was that you keep a fucking eye on her. Not find her something to fuck."

He glanced to the hallway, listening for Cody's laughter, Jazz's booming voice.

"Well, we just went ahead and did both for you." Zack's smile was all teeth. "And just look at all the thank-yous we're getting." His gaze snapped with ire. "You're a damned fool, Slade. You should have told Jessie the truth starting out, instead of leaving her the way you did. And what the hell? Did you forget how to use a condom?"

Slade tossed back another fiery swallow of the whisky. "I was drunk," he snarled. "That fucking wedding and reception, and all I could think about was Jessie. All I could feel or see was Jessie. Amy very conveniently took advantage of it. More than once."

Those first months had been worse than hell. He came in at night, after dealing with Kingston and Baines and their self-glorified gloating over what excellent businessmen they were. He would get quietly, calmly, as drunk as hell. And Amy being Amy wasn't one to let an opportunity slip by. According to Amy just before her death, getting him in her bed was imperative. He wasn't Cody's father, and she could never let anyone discover that. It would not only foul the operation, but it would jeopardize her plans as well. Hers and her lover's.

Slade sat in one of the kitchen chairs, lowering his head as he wiped his hands wearily over his face. He had never forgiven Amy for that, for getting pregnant during such a dangerous mission. She hadn't wanted a child, and according to her, didn't love the father. Her goal had been to project the perfect family to lure Kingston and Baines into the trap so that they could trust Slade. What she was really after was stealing that fucking money so she and her lover could escape.

Zack grunted, stomping away as he pulled his cell phone free of his jeans and began making his calls, checking to see if anyone had seen Jessie. Slade listened with a heavy heart. How many times was Jessie going to let him hurt her before she gave up? Before the love that filled her soul was destroyed forever.

"She's just driving around." He flipped the phone closed long minutes later. "She's fine, Slade. She's not speeding or acting foolish, like some people we know have been prone to do." He shot Slade an accusing look.

Slade nodded slowly, his head turning as the door to the bedroom could be heard opening and Cody came racing out, dressed in a woman's small T-shirt.

"Jessie left a few things here awhile back." Jazz grinned. "Tiniest little woman I ever laid my eyes on."

Slade stared at the T-shirt. It swallowed his son. Slade's eyes lifted to Jazz's then. The implication of Jessie's clothes being there was clear, but he couldn't find the energy to be enraged. Jazz didn't love Jessie. Any man who loved her would never give her up so easily. Jazz had done though, just as Slade had asked of him. He had saved Jessie for him. Taken care of her. Kept her from rebounding with another man and destroying both their souls.

Some things men just didn't talk about though. As Slade stared back at his friend he let a smile edge his lips as he nodded softly. Yeah, he and Jazz were fine with this.

Jazz's return nod settled it. They were good. Brothers. Just like they had always been.

"Daddy. Jazz said the lady that pulled me out was your girlfriend." Cody snickered teasingly, dimples forming at his cheeks as he jumped into Slade's lap. "If she's your girlfriend, is she gonna be my momma?"

Hell yes she was.

"Settle down, Cody. We'll talk about mommas later." He pulled his son against his chest, stroking his hand down his back. For all his present cheerfulness, there were fine tremors still shaking through Cody's body.

Slade fought not to crush him in his arms, to keep from clutching at him, to still the grief rising inside him.

Glenna's vindictiveness had nearly killed her own daughter's child. Her hatred of Jessie, and evidently Slade as well, had almost destroyed all their lives. It was something he wouldn't let pass. He wouldn't be able to get to her now, Jazz and Zack were like damned mother hens sometimes. But he would get to her.

"Me and Cody are going to go after that ice cream and make a little pit stop at the clinic," Jazz announced. "Make sure that ole lake water ain't gonna stunt his growth."

Slade shook his head. His kid. He didn't need anyone else taking care of his boy any more than he needed anyone else taking care of his woman. At least, not in the important areas.

"I'll take him." Bone-deep sadness filled his soul as the truth of what had happened began sinking into him. "What do you think, Son? Will ice cream and chips make up for the doctor?"

"Cookies too." Cody nodded at the thought. "Good cookies. But you're still wet, Daddy."

The kid ate like a little pig and never gained a pound. He had to be the scrawniest scrap of a guy for his age that Slade had ever laid his eyes on. And the boy was right, he was still wet. Sighing, Slade lifted the boy to Zack, marveling once again at how tiny the boy was. For a kid who ate so much, he should be three times his size.

"Jazz will just follow along then and make sure you don't head places you shouldn't be. I'll stay here and talk to J.J. when he arrives," Zack announced.

Jesse James Roberts was the sheriff and an old friend. Slade rose to his feet, running his fingers through his hair as he headed to the spare room and the change of clothes he kept there. He didn't argue Zack's announcement. He was afraid himself he'd end up killing Glenna. His control was shot.

After a quick shower and change of clothes, Slade stepped back into the kitchen, whisking Cody from the floor where he and Jazz and been wrestling, and holding him close to his chest.

"Come on, little man." He kissed Cody's head as he headed for the door. "Let's go find you some clean clothes and then Daddy will get you that ice cream and cookies. But we're going to go see that nice doctor we saw last week. How does that sound?"

"Okay." Cody sighed, obviously put out at the thought of the nice doctor. "Then, I want to meet your girlfriend. I need a momma, Daddy. They make good cookies. You burn yours."

Slade winced as Jazz snickered behind him. Sold out for a cookie. Now wasn't that just about typical of how his life was going lately?

Chapter Twenty

Slade wasn't at the apartment when she pulled into the parking lot and stared at the small lake the tributary from the nearby river created. Zack's pickup was gone, but Jazz's flashy '69 Corvcttc was sitting in front of thc doorway that led to the upstairs apartments.

Dragging herself wearily from the car, Jessie moved slowly to the doorway and upstairs. She was exhausted, her mind running in circles, the years of hating, longing and hurting had culminated to this one point. In the time it had taken for her to see one little boy toppling into the water, to hearing Slade's pleas for God's mercy and his son's life.

What had happened? She remembered Amy bragging that week that Slade was hers, that he would always be hers. Jessie remembered her panic at hearing of the confidence in the other woman's voice. Had she somehow unconsciously known that Amy was pregnant?

Shaking her head at her inability to answer the question, she unlocked the apartment and stepped in, suspecting what she would find there. And there was

Jazz, slouched back in her favorite chair, a soda in his hand as he watched her television.

"'Bout time you dragged that little ass in," he grunted as he sat up, almost setting the can on her end-table before grimacing, rising to his feet and heading to the kitchen. The last time he left a can on her end-table, he had worn the soda home.

"Good boy," she muttered as she dropped her keys into the purse sitting on the table by the door and moved through the house. "Now go home where you belong."

"Aw hell, Jessie. You can't run me off." He sighed as he walked back into the living room. "You know that shit don't work."

That was the truth. He had shadowed her like a bad smell for the past five years. Him and Zack both.

She stared at him, seeing the worry that edged his eyes, that tightened his sensual lips. Jazz was a damned fine-looking man. Six-foot-five, a wild man of black hair that flowed to his shoulders, and ice-blue eyes. Jazz was a complete sensualist, a hedonist. In that, he was a lot like Slade and she suspected Zack as well. But where the other two men partially hid that extreme sexuality, Jazz reveled in it. Something Jessie hadn't been able to fully appreciate the few times she had shared his bed.

"Why?" She watched him curiously, wondering why he had put himself and his friendship with Slade on the line by sleeping with her.

He didn't ask what she meant, he knew. He raked his fingers through his hair as he turned back to her, his expression more serious than she had seen it in a long time.

"You belonged to Slade." He finally shrugged. "You knew that, even if you wanted to deny it, and so did I. And you were hurting."

"Why, Jazz?" she asked again, giving him the look she gave her students when she knew the truth wasn't exactly coming out.

"Hell, Jess. He's my bud," he snapped, his blue eyes flaming. "You were his girl. You didn't need to fall in love; you just needed someone to pretend with you a time or two. Slade knows that. We don't discuss it and we won't, but Slade knows or he would have killed me instead of just bitching about it a little bit."

And to Jazz she knew that explained it all. They were, essentially, his family. Slade, Jazz and Zack had something important in common. The three of them were foster children, unwanted children. The rules seemed to morph for children who had been raised with the feeling they were castoffs, that they had no one. Slade, Jazz and Zack had bonded as friends in the boys' school they had been sheltered at in town; fostered out to different families, they were each other's stability. Family.

Jessie moved over to a nearby chair and sat down slowly, her stomach twisting with the sickening realization of the stress she must have placed on that friendship, that bond Slade and Jazz shared.

"I'm sorry," she whispered, holding back the tears that threatened once again.

"Sweet pea, you have no reason to be apologizin'." He sighed as he bent in front of her, his large hand moving beneath her chin to tip her face up to his. "I offered. I made myself available, and I made sure none of those dumb pricks panting after you had a chance. You needed sugar, and I provided." He smiled slowly, gently. "And I saved you for my brother, just like he would have done for me if the position had been reversed."

"And you?" she whispered painfully. "You risked your friendship, someone important to you, to save me."

"Naw." He shook his head firmly. "I talked to Slade while he was gone, sweetheart. I knew how he was hurting, how he worried about you. How he wanted you happy. Slade's a good guy, Jess. And that man loves you more than life. And he loves me. He knows who I held you for, and that's all that matters to him."

Jessie swallowed tightly. "I love you, Jazz," she whispered, and knew it was true. It wasn't a romantic love, or a sexual love. He was, next to Slade, one of the dearest people in her life though.

"Sweet pea, I love you too." He leaned forward and kissed her check with all the affection of an older brother. "And everything's going to be okay. I'll let Slade know you're home before he goes insane. Zack is gonna stay with little Cody and he'll come to you..."

"No." She shook her head fiercely as she moved to her feet.

"Jess, you can't let him pace all night, worrying—"

"I have to go to him." She swung to Jazz as he stood slowly, watching her quietly. "It's my turn, Jazz. I have to go to Slade."

His smile was warm, tender. "Maybe you're right." He finally nodded, then winked. "Take a shower first though, sweet pea. You're pretty as a picture, but dried river water ain't the nicest smell."

"No." Her nose wrinkled as she lifted the hem of her cover-up and sniffed. "It's not the best smell."

"I'll head downstairs and keep answering his every thirty-minute calls." Jazz sighed as though put upon. "The things I do for you, beauty. Just the things I do."

A smile tugged at her lips as he walked from the apartment to the symphony of his cell phone ringing imperatively.

"She ain't home yet, dude." His voice was muffled as the door closed. "Hang onto your breeches, I'll let you know when she gets here..."

Chapter Twenty-one

Slade's house was just as beautiful as it had been five years before. A two-story farmhouse with rough wood siding and a wrap-around porch, the masculine elegance and charm of the home had drawn her from the moment she had seen it.

He had cleaned it up a lot. It had been overgrown, the yard waist-high in weeds and grass. It was now well cut, the wood fence running around the perimeter glistened with a coat of dark brown stain that matched the house. It was a family house. The type of house meant to be filled with children's laughter and the smell of fresh baked pies.

For now, it was quiet. Slade's jeep was parked in the cemented driveway beside Zack's pickup; the porch light was on, welcoming the coming nightfall, and through the open living-room shades she could see him pacing with the phone to his ear.

With her headlights turned off, and the sky just turning toward night, Jessie drove her gray compact into the driveway, parking beside Zack's truck. She breathed out a hard sigh. This was hard. One of the hardest things she had ever done in her life. She was coming to Slade. No games, no pretenses as there had been that first time five years ago. She was coming to him, openly.

She was terrified. She knew he loved her. Slade wasn't a man to play games and she had always known that, despite her attempts to hide from it or to tell herself otherwise.

It was pride. He had broken her heart when he walked out, but even then Jessie had known in the back of her mind that he wasn't leaving because he wanted to. She had seen the grief in his eyes, the wild hunger and loss that had creased his face. But all she heard were the words, the rejection. And it was all she had let herself remember.

Drawing in a deep breath, she opened the car door and stepped out. The wide front door jerked open and Slade moved onto the porch. Jessie stopped by her car, shaking, trembling as his brooding stare locked on her, his expression shadowed in the dim light, his big body tense as Zack joined him.

Slapping Slade on the shoulder, Zack moved past him, his concerned gaze on Jessie as he moved to his pickup. Jessie closed the door of her car and met him as he crossed the driveway.

"You okay, sweetheart?" His voice was low as he stopped in front of her, his green eyes filled with worry.

"I'm fine." She winced at the scratchiness of her voice, a product of the tears she had shed through the day.

She tucked her hands into her jeans as she glanced over his shoulder to where Slade watched them silently. "Is he okay?"

Zack looked back before turning to her again with a soft smile. "He and the boy are doing good, honey. You did good. How are you?"

She nodded slowly. "I'm good. But I have to talk to him now."

The need to know was burning inside her, but the need for explanations wasn't all that tore at her heart. She had to make certain the little boy, Cody, was okay.

"Good luck, sweetheart." Zack pulled her to his chest, placed a kiss of the top of her head and then moved away.

Jessie kept her head down, fighting back more tears. Jazz and Zack had saved her after Slade had left. She hadn't been mature enough, hadn't guarded enough of her heart to pull herself out of the bleak pain that had suffused her. With her family gone there had been no one to go to, no one to ease the void that grew within her until they stepped in.

"Later, Zack," she whispered at his truck door, and moved to the walk that led to Slade's front porch.

He hadn't spoken, he just watched her. In his eyes she saw the same pain that had raged there five years ago, the night he had walked out of her life and entered Amy's. But this time, she also saw the love in them, the emotion, the certain way he looked at her that he never used with anyone else. The way he had looked at her since she was sixteen years old.

She stopped at the first step, staring up at him with her heart in her throat. He had every right to ask her to leave, to turn his back on her.

"Can I come in?" She stilled the trembling of her lips as she stood before him, uncertain what to say, what to do.

"It's your house, Jessie." He moved back, stepping aside as she moved up to the porch. "I've been worried about you."

He didn't touch her with anything but his eyes. Eyes that caressed her, that stole her breath.

"I needed to think." She hunched her shoulders against his questioning look as he opened the front storm door and let her step inside. "About a lot of things."

The inside of the house was as yet undecorated. A few pieces of furniture graced the living room, but the dining room was bare. The kitchen held appliances and a small wooden table.

She had never been inside his home, but as she stared around from the entryway, the wide-open rooms, sense of space—and waiting—struck her. It was a house waiting to be a home, with a small start already begun in the few toys she saw scattered around the living room.

Stepping into the room, she picked up the little stuffed bear, testing the softness of it before she laid it in the large plastic toy chest against the wall. There were several plastic trucks and cars, made for little hands, parked haphazardly against the front of the television. She picked those up as well.

As she laid them in the toy chest, she stared into the inside, feeling Slade close behind her, watching her.

"He's just a little boy," she whispered. "My mom always said boys were so much harder to raise than girls.

You have to teach them things young. Like putting away their toys and stuff." She glanced back at him with a bittersweet smile. "I have a brother, you know. He doesn't live around here. He's in the service."

"I know your brother, Jessie." He tilted his head, watching her carefully. "He was very firm when he reminded me of your age before he went into the service."

She looked back at him in surprise.

"You were sixteen." His expression was somber, though his lips kicked up in a small grin. "He threatened to castrate me."

"Yeah, that sounds like Benji." She drew in a deep breath as she stood up and stared around the room before coming back to his gaze. "We need to talk, Slade. About five years ago. About Cody." She turned back to him, pulling in a deep breath and stealing herself for the truth. "Was Amy pregnant with Cody when you married her?"

She watched as he drew in a deep, hard breath.

"I didn't marry Amy because she was pregnant," he finally answered. "I married Amy because she was my partner in a very sensitive operation we were involved in back in D.C. Amy and I were agents for the Office of Homeland Security, Jessie."

She had to sit down. Jessie stumbled to a nearby chair before staring back at Slade in shock as he raked his fingers through his hair in frustration. His eyes were stormy with emotion as he moved over to the chair beside her. Jerking it from its position against the wall, he set it in front of her before sitting down, his gaze locked with hers.

"I was recruited first by the F.B.I. while I was in college." He leaned closer to her, his hands hanging between his spread legs, close to her knees.

As she stared down at them, he moved his index finger, running it gently over her jean-clad knee.

"After 9/11, some of us were placed under the jurisdiction of the Office of Homeland Security. Amy and I were two of those agents. We were working undercover to infiltrate a group of arms dealers selling weapons in the Middle East. When I came home five years ago, it was after the operation had supposedly been dropped. We were getting nowhere." He breathed out roughly, the sigh of air ruffling against the top of her head as her chest tightened with fear.

"What happened?"

He picked up her hand. Her fingers looked fragile, protected within his larger, stronger grip.

"The organization we were investigating had a 'family values' stand." He snorted. "Amy and I had announced an engagement before the operation was stalled. We were told it was over. I came home. The weekend we spent together, Amy had received a message from the head of the organization. He wanted to host the wedding. We were being let in..." His fingers rubbed against her ring finger. "We had to go through with it. Pulling back then would have placed not just our own lives in danger but the lives of our families. Those we loved. It wasn't a friendly organization if they thought you were screwing them around." His voice roughened, the grief that had pierced her soul when he left echoed in it.

Jessie lifted her head, battling the tears she realized had begun to fall from her eyes.

"Jessie." His expression twisted into a grimace of pain as his hands framed her face. "I loved you, baby. I loved you past everything I knew, but they had to come down. The weapons killing our men in the Middle East were being sold to them by Americans. That weighed enough on my conscience, but the men we were investigating had sent someone here to check us out, to watch us. I couldn't risk everyone I loved. I couldn't risk you."

Jessie fought back the sob threatening to tear through her chest. Could she have done that? Could she have walked away from her own wants and needs to act so selflessly?

"Amy's pregnancy?"

He shook his head wearily. "I was drunk, and she was desperate. She told me just before the operation went to hell that Cody wasn't mine." His lips twisted bitterly. "By then, it didn't matter, Jessie. That's my boy, blood or not."

Jessie frowned. She had pictures of Slade when he was a child that her mother had taken while her father had been principal at Slade's school. She wasn't positive, but pretty certain there was no way Cody could belong to anyone else.

But where did that leave them now?

Slade watched Jessie shake her head before dropping it to her knees and breathing in roughly. She broke his heart—she made his heart beat. She breathed life into his soul and dreams of her were often all that kept him warm at night in the past five years.

What was he supposed to say to her now, he wondered. How was he supposed to make what he had done any easier for her to bear?

"I think I knew all along," she whispered, her voice muffled as she kept her forehead pressed against her knees. "I just didn't want to face it. I couldn't let myself believe that you loved me, that you regretted leaving, even though I knew. I knew that night in Jazz's RV wasn't a dream. I knew it was killing you even then, just as much as it was me, but I couldn't face it. If I had to face it, I couldn't have lived."

Slade swallowed tightly, feeling old, broken as he listened to her tear-filled voice.

"I had hope," she whispered as he frowned down at her. "As long as I let myself believe it was because I was immature, too young, I had hope you'd come home, realize I had grown up and everything would be fixed. Then you came home. Amy was gone, and I couldn't do anything. I was still terrified, still so uncertain. And I still loved you so much..." She lifted her head, staring back at him miserably. "But I couldn't let go. Because if I let go then I had to admit the truth. And if I did that, then I would have to face betraying you..." Her voice broke, tears filling her eyes as he watched her in shock. "I would have to admit I betrayed that love..." A tear slipped free. "Even though I knew, all the way to my soul I knew you loved me, I still slept with Jazz, I let myself hate you...I had to hate you to survive..."

"God. Jessie, no..." He jumped from his chair, his hands gripping her forearms, pulling her roughly from her chair to stare down at her furiously. "Don't you do this to yourself." He shook her, gently. "Do you think I blame you? Do you think for a minute, baby, that I didn't do what I did so you would hate me? So you could go on?" His throat was tight with emotion, his chest aching with it. "I thought you were asleep when I came to Jazz's RV. I didn't even think you would know I was there. Baby, you didn't do anything wrong."

Her face spasmed as she fought to hold back her sobs. The tears trickled down her cheeks as she pushed away from him, wrapping her arms around her breasts.

"You were mine." The snarl in her voice had him frowning, uncertain. "You were mine and she gave you the child I prayed for. She was bragging the week before that, that you were hers. That she would have you." A bitter laugh left her lips. "God, I think I knew even then that somehow I was going to lose you. So I slipped into the RV and I hid in your bed, knowing you weren't going to come to me. Knowing you would hide. I knew..." Her hands fell to her side, her fists clenching so tight they paled as Slade watched her, listened to her, the weight in his soul lifting with each word. "But you were mine!" She turned back to him, her expression fierce, her eyes glinting with anger now. "So I hid and I waited and I teased you into taking me, knowing...I knew what was coming and I still blamed you. I still hated you and like a goddamned baby I closed my eyes and jumped right into my own fucking misery rather than accepting it."

God, she was going to be a handful. Slade stared back at her, hiding the joy exploding from his chest. Not because she had been miserable, not because he knew what he had suspected all along, that his sweet little Jessie had deliberately tried to seduce him, had lied about being asleep on the RV rather than admitting she had all intention of taking her man.

Hell no. His heart was beating; his entire being was freed knowing, seeing in her eyes the fierce, possessive streak of steel-strong devotion he felt for her.

He crossed his arms over his chest, frowning down at her as she met his gaze, the flames of her anger warming him faster than a bonfire.

"So you set out to seduce me?" He kept his voice from revealing the complete pleasure tearing through him.

"You're damned right I did," she snapped, her brown eyes glittering fiercely. "I waited on you since I was sixteen years old and figured out how damned good a man's hands could feel against my skin. Your hands, the night of my birthday when you danced with me. I felt your hands against my back, your fingers making those little moves on my skin like you were trying to get beneath it. You were aroused," she accused him harshly. "You did everything to hide it but I know you were."

God yes, she had been sweet sixteen and as sexy as hell. She had tempted him to a point that had almost terrified him. He thanked God when his vacation was up that summer, knowing if he didn't get away from her, he was going to end up in jail. Because nothing would have stopped him from taking her.

She dashed at the tears on her cheeks, staring at him defensively as she drew in a deep breath, her top pressing against her breasts, daring him to rip it off her.

"So you just deliberately teased me all those years?" He lifted his brow.

God, he was going to paddle her bottom. She had no idea the hell she put him through.

"You and Jazz and Zack thought I was so innocent." She rolled her eyes expressively, glaring at him. "I was a virgin, Slade, not stupid. I knew what a hard-on was and what it was for and I knew if my own fingers could make me feel good then yours would destroy me with pleasure. I wasn't stupid. But I loved you." The fury on her face almost made him step back. Damn, she looked like Rhonda before she got the frying pan out. "And you were fucking a path through three damned counties like a buck in heat," she snarled. "I think I did hate you for that."

Slade fought the flush rising in his face. Yeah, he had. It was that or fuck her.

"I'm going to spank you, Jessie." He watched the shock fill her face. "I'm going to paddle your ass until it's beet-red then flip you over and make you show me exactly how you made yourself feel so good."

Jessie stared at him in shock.

"Have you heard a single word I've said to you?" she threw at him, anger still surging inside her. "Slade, I seduced you. I put you through hell thinking this was all your fault and you're going to fuck me for it? Oh yeah, big punishment there, stud."

His eyes flared at the title, the gray depths darkening, his cheeks flushing with lust.

"I heard you, Jezebel," he grunted. "Let's see, what should I do with a woman who deliberately gave me the most incredible weekend of sex I've ever had? Who filled my soul with light and gave me a reason to believe in the love I never thought existed?"

He tilted his head, watching her eyes widen.

"I think I should fuck you. First your sweet, tight pussy, then that hot little ass until you beg me for forgiveness. Maybe both at once." He nodded sharply. "That should teach you your lesson."

"Slade?" She licked her lips nervously, watching him, misery battling with hope. "Don't you understand what I did? I slept with Jazz. I hated you..."

He shook his head, breathing roughly. "I still want to castrate that damned farm boy for touching you, Jessie, stop reminding me." He reached out, brushed back a fringe of hair and smiled with a gentleness that wrapped around her heart and healed the pain that had throbbed there for so long. "But, baby, I thank God in the same breath it was Jazz. I didn't ask him to hold you for me. I didn't ask any of them to do anything but keep me from prison by not letting any of those half-witted pricks who pushed and shoved to get next to you, into your bed. I would have killed one of them."

She stood still, silent, as he moved closer to her, his hands framing her face, a small smile tilting his lips.

"I loved you, Jessie, even before I let you seduce me. I loved you until I was fucking a path through three counties in an attempt to keep from killing you once I got my dick inside you. You terrified the hell out of me and drew me like a moth to a flame. If that weekend held your heart while that fiasco with Amy played out, then all the better. I deserved to suffer for being so brick-dumb in the first place. But you didn't."

He lowered his head, his lips smoothing over hers as they trembled, as she stared at him in disbelief.

"I've loved you since you were sixteen, all big eyes and lush, sweet lips. That night we danced, I marked you as mine and I made it stick. There wasn't a boy or a man on that lake that didn't know who you belonged to, and the minute there was even a whiff one of them was stepping over the line, they walked funny for a week."

Her eyes widened, memories sweeping over her. The last two years of high school when getting a date was like pulling teeth. After that, the way men shied away from her after coming on hard enough to gain notice.

Her eyes narrowed.

"That was dirty."

"And what you told Melissa Loring wasn't?" He lifted his brow as she felt horror sweep over her.

She swallowed tightly. "She told you?"

"She didn't have to tell me." He chuckled, the sound wicked and all too sexy. "Her brother told Jazz when she asked him if you really owned a gun and if he thought you were ballsy enough use it."

Jessie ducked her head, a flush staining her cheeks.

"She was a floozy," she accused in embarrassment. "Bragging to me about the things she could do with your hard body. At least Amy had the good sense to stay the hell away from me."

His thumbs smoothed over her cheeks as she laid her palms tentatively against his abdomen.

"I don't want to grow up, Slade," she whispered. "I don't want to worry about being sophisticated and wearing damned makeup all the time and wearing the right shoes. But I will. I'll do it. But that's not me..."

"Jessie baby." He groaned, a teasing smile crossing his lips. "You look like a dream no matter how you're dressed and I don't give a damn what you wear. If you hadn't noticed, even before, the social bullshit didn't pull me. We'll do what we have to do, then come home, shuck the glad rags and pull on our shorts and be ourselves. Sweetheart, you're what I want. Wearing makeup or not. Naked or dressed. Though, I'd go for naked as often as possible. I love you, Jessie. Every sweet inch of you, inside and out."

"I love you, Slade. I always loved you."

Slade felt the sweet relief rushing through his system even as his blood began to pound with lust. It was sweeping through him, eating at his guts as his cock jerked to full throbbing strength, pressing against his jeans and demanding release.

Jessie was staring at him with stars in her eyes, her expression easing from the bitter, grief-stricken pain of moments before as she let his words sink in.

"You should be angry with me," she said softly. "I may have gotten older, but I didn't get a whole lot wiser, Slade."

Hadn't she?

"You waited for me," he whispered. "Admit it, Jessie. You did something I never believed was possible for a woman to do for a man. You waited for me. You saved your heart, and despite that damned Jazz, you saved your body." He leaned his forehead against hers. "Who did you think about when he touched you, baby? When he was holding you, whose arms did you feel? Who was loving you?"

"You. Always you." Sweet innocence. It filled her eyes, shaped her expression. She was like a breath of early morning air, soft and untainted, as sweetly innocent as life itself.

"And it was the same for me." His heart clenched at the years they had lost. "I dreamed of you, I held you. Amy claimed the title, but in my heart, you were my wife, Jessie. Forever and always. I won't regret the past. I can't regret Cody. I love that boy. But we have our chance now. I want to grab it with both hands, hold on tight and claim everything we lost the first time."

"I still think you've been an ass," she pouted prettily. "You should have told me about Cody, Slade. That first night, you should have explained."

"Yeah, I should have." He kissed her forehead, pulling her to his lap as he sat back in the chair, his arms going around her. "I wanted you to accept me first, Jessie, before I asked you to accept a child another woman bore. I wanted to be sure, before I got Cody's hopes up." His son needed a mother. Amy had failed as dismally there as he had failed as a husband.

Jessie curled into his arms now, her hand lying against his chest, her head resting on his shoulder as he let his hands rove over her. He wanted her until he had to force himself to breathe, but God this was good. Just holding her, feeling the silence of the evening wrapping around them, feeling her, soul deep, so much a part of him he knew he couldn't survive without her touch.

"He's really okay?" she whispered. "You took him to Dr. Gladmore's clinic right? Old Doc Morrison shouldn't be treating dogs, let alone children. You should have found a pediatrician to oversee him when you first got home."

Slade let a smile tug at his lips.

"I didn't know that." He kissed her neck gently, reverently. "Maybe you could kind of help me out there some."

She was silent long enough that he began to get worried.

"Doctor Stephens..." She named a doctor in a neighboring county. "She's a good pediatrician. My sister used to take her kids there, before they moved. I'll call and make him an appointment. Have you enrolled him in school yet? It starts soon, and I'd like to have a chance to

239

make certain he goes into the right room. Getting with the proper teacher means everything, Slade. I want you to come to the school the first of the week and get him enrolled."

"Hmm. You'll help me with that too?" He nuzzled at her ear as she nodded briskly.

"I'll go in with you. Clarissa is a damned bitch, but hopefully she'll be nice to family..."

Slade sighed regretfully, worrying now. "Glenna dropped him off at the dock, Jessie. She pointed him to the offices and just left after she saw me coming out of the door that led to the apartments. She left him out there deliberately. She knows you live here too, and guessed where I had been."

Jessie tensed, then began to shake with fury as she turned to stare at him incredulously, her eyes wide, shocked.

"Is she still breathing?" Her voice was rough with rage. "Because if she is, she won't be for much longer."

His arms tightened around the little wildcat. Damn, he loved her.

"J.J.'s taking care of it, Jessie. I won't press charges, but don't trust Clarissa too damned far. Maybe we'll move him to one of the other schools."

She shook her head slowly, thoughtfully. "No, I'll take care of him. I know the teacher I want him with and Clarissa doesn't mess with me. She knows I'll pull every hair in her head out if she does. She just pisses me off. She's a lousy principal."

Slade sat silently. He could hear her thinking, feel her making plans and it radiated through him like sunlight. She would accept Cody, and she would be a hell of a mother.

He finally sighed. "Cody's not my biological child, Jessie but..."

She stared back at him, silent, disbelieving.

He glanced away for a long moment. "He's still my kid..."

"You let her lie to you like that?" she asked. "You know, Slade, I admit, I can have tunnel vision at times, but I think you just shut the lights off. What the hell do you mean he's not your biological child? There's not a chance in hell that child could belong to anyone else."

Jessie remembered looking at him, seeing the turquoise eyes as they jerked open, that wild mop of dark curls. And he was so damned scraggly he looked like he never ate. She bet he ate like a herd of elephants after a drought.

"He doesn't look like me or Amy." He snorted. "She told me when she left..."

"Come here." She knew better than to argue with Slade when he was convinced of something. You had to show him proof, and that was something she had.

She moved from his lap and walked to where she had dropped her purse at the hall table. She had pulled the pictures out while she was in her apartment, not certain why she needed to see the old photos of Slade as a child. To be certain herself maybe. She had taken them from her mother during one of her odd visits to Florida. "Dad was the principal at the school, remember?" She pulled the photos free as she walked back to him. "Mom was always taking pictures of the kids for the yearbooks. Especially those kids whose parents never bought their school pictures. She was a fanatic."

She lifted the most revealing photo from the pile. Slade, at Cody's age, scrawny as hell, his dark brown hair wild with curls, his turquoise eyes somber as he stared back from the picture. Her mother had always loved the children without parents best.

"Do you remember Mom?" she asked him.

"I remember her." His lips tilted into a grin. "I remember your dad too." His frown was the same of any other boy who had ever gone to school during her dad's reign. "And his paddle." Yep. He remembered her dad.

"Look at this." She handed him the picture, watching his eyes widen, flare with shock, his face slacken in surprise before his gaze lifted to her.

"Don't you have any pictures of yourself when you were little?" It was criminal that he shouldn't.

He shook his head slowly. "No one took pictures."

"Well, Mom did." She handed him the rest. "From kindergarten to the seventh grade, Slade. Your looks began changing when you hit high school. The dark blue of your eyes lightening, your body starting to fill out. You were one of those kids who just didn't look the same as you got older. I suspect Cody will follow you."

Slade blinked, going through the pictures, his throat tightening with emotion at the proof that Cody was indeed his son. Not just because Slade loved him, because he was a part of Slade.

"Amy was a mean bitch." She sat in the chair in front of him, breathing out deeply. "You knew that before you fucked her," she griped disdainfully. "You couldn't trust a word she said."

"She used Cody," he said bitterly. "The organization was run by fanatics. I couldn't reach the upper levels without the required family. Something for them to threaten, to hold over a man's head. Amy decided to take the risk of losing a child if the operation went to hell."

Jessie lowered her head, her hands gripped in her lap as she nodded slowly. Yeah, that sounded like Amy. She was the type of woman who made certain all her demands were met her way. And she had wanted Slade, operation or not.

"Damn, I was scrawny." He sighed as he went through the photos. "I was starting to worry about Cody. That kid eats like a horse and never seems to grow an inch. I swear, some days I think he's going to bankrupt me in food. His voice was full of love, whispery-soft with his devotion to his son.

"Well, you're not a lightweight yourself," she grunted. "I've seen you eat, Slade. You would put a horse to shame."

She glanced up in time to see his smile, thankful, adoring, filled with a very male, very possessive love. It sent heat spiraling through her, made her breasts swell, her nipples rasp against the soft material of her T-shirt.

"Damn." His face clenched, a grimace of emotion twisting his features. "He's just like me, huh?"

"Just like you," she answered softly, and for a moment, just a moment, that sadness that the child he loved so dearly wasn't hers as well, nearly overwhelmed her.

"He needs a momma, you know." He cleared his throat, laying the pictures aside before turning back to face her. "I want you to marry me, Jessie. I didn't come back here to play games or waste more time without you in my bed where you belong, every night. I suck at romance and I know it. I wanted to give you the ring first, wanted to ease you into this, make everything right." He touched her face, another of those caresses that sped through her body, clenching her heart with joy. There was nothing so perfect as when Slade touched her.

Her eyes filled with tears. "I never want to lose you again," she whispered. "I've been yours since I was sixteen, Slade. Always yours."

"That's a yes, then?" He arched his brow, devilish, seductive humor creeping into his gray eyes.

"Yeah," she sighed, joy exploding inside her. "That's a yes, Slade."

As though she could have said anything else.

Chapter Twenty-two

The sound of her soft voice, accepting him, accepting his child so easily sent a pulse of pure emotion exploding in Slade's chest. His breath caught with the incandescence of her smile, the love in her eyes.

She didn't want to grow up, she said. By God, if growing up meant she lost the waif-like innocence and steel-hard core of determination, then he'd beat her if she grew up.

Before he considered anything else though, he had to have her. Rising to his feet, before Jessie could do more than gasp, Slade had her in his arms, stalking to the one place in the house he knew his Jesse could scream without little ears hearing her. The downstairs bedroom was well insulated, more because Slade had a habit of playing his old electric guitar as loud as the amplifier would go. Insulating the spare guest room had been his one concession to it.

As he closed and locked the door behind them, he pulled a small receiver from his back pocket, looked at it, flipped a switch and laid it beside the bed. Jessie looked back at him in question.

"Cody locator," he grunted. "I had to install electronic strips around the doorways and at the stairwell to let me know when he passes through it. He likes to wander around by himself if he gets up before I do."

Yeah, she remembered her brother doing that. Shoot, they had all done it.

"God, I can't believe I have you here, Jess," Slade whispered, his hands smoothing up her arms, pulling her closer as the big bed loomed beside them. "I've dreamed of having you here. Loving you. Touching you."

Tangling his fingers in her hair, he lowered his head, taking her lips in a kiss that threatened to make his knees weak. Long, sipping kisses, a tangle of lips caressing, tasting, smoothing over each other as he moaned at the rippling effects of heat chasing through his system.

His cock was iron hard, pounding beneath his jeans as he toed at his boots, working them off slowly, one by one. He tasted Jessie, nipped at her lips then soothed the little sting with a lick of his tongue. But he was a hungry man. One taste of her, one feel of those sweet curves and his tongue was a greedy bastard. It slipped into her mouth, delving into the dark honey taste as she met him with hers and the pleasure began to consume them.

Within minutes his boots were kicked across the floor and Jessie was wiggling from her sneakers and jeans as she fought to hold onto his kiss. He gripped the neckline of her T-shirt and just ripped it off. He didn't have the patience for careful seduction. Not this time.

"You keep destroying my clothes," she moaned as his lips moved from hers, his teeth raking across her neck while he dealt with her panties in the same fashion.

"Then stop wearing the damned things," he growled as her hands tore at his shirt, popping buttons in her desperation to get him undressed.

God, he was going to come in his jeans if he didn't get inside her hot body. She made him so fucking horny he felt as though he were going to go up in flames. Sweat covered his body before he managed to shrug the tattered remains of his shirt from his shoulders, while her mouth was attacking his flesh. Fuck, her tongue licked over his flat, hard nipples, her sharp little teeth nipping at them wickedly as he looked down at her, seeing the sensuality transforming her features.

"You're being a bad girl." He groaned as her tongue curled around the dark disc it was tormenting. He hadn't taught her shit, that left only one person. "You think I don't know who taught you this shit?"

"Hmm, you taught me," she whispered, surprising him. "You make me so crazy when you do this. I want to make you just as crazy."

His stomach tightened at the thought of having her experiment on him, testing out the caresses he had given her on his tougher body. Just the thought of it had his balls tightening, his cock twitching.

"You like that thought, stud?" Her hand curled between his thighs, cupping the aching spheres as she wiggled against him.

"You keep calling me stud and I'm going to show what one is good for," he grunted. "You're playing with a desperate man here, Jessie."

"Am I playing?" She knelt between his thighs, her fingers moving along his erection as he gritted his teeth with the pleasure.

"Shit." He was almost panting for air now.

"Easy does it, stud." She smiled, a slow, easy, sexy as fucking hell curve of her lips as his hands moved to the waistband of his jeans. If he didn't get the restrictive material off his ass, it was going to strangle his dick.

She brushed his hands away, her silken fingers moving against his convulsing abdomen as she loosened the snap of the low-slung denim.

"I missed you, Slade." She leaned forward, planting a kiss on the skin revealed by the loosened waistband as his hands buried in her hair.

"God, baby," he moaned, swallowing tightly as her inquisitive little tongue licked at his flesh while her fingers lowered the zipper over his pounding cock. "If you don't move the schedule up here a bit, the game is going to be over."

"Mmm. Like you don't stay hard for hours," she whispered a second before her teeth nipped at his lower abs, causing a silent snarl of agonized pleasure to tighten his lips.

"I stay hard for you period." He was almost panting as the jeans loosened and her graceful fingers curled into the waistband.

He lifted, his fingers clenching at his side as he let her draw his jeans and briefs down his hips. His cock raked her lips and her tongue swiped at it as though in chastisement, pulling a strangled moan from his chest.

There was no convincing here, no seduction. She was moving over him like honey, her hands pulling his jeans away as she knelt naked before him, her tongue curling around the head of his erection. She was making him insane. His balls were agonized they were pulled so damned tight against the base of his cock, his entire body wracked by pleasure as she tossed his jeans aside then bent to the tortured spheres.

"Sweet God in Heaven..." His head fell back, his fingers clenching in her hair as she sucked at the sensitized pouch, licking, her teeth raking, her sweet fucking tongue... Ah God, her tongue was killing him.

Then her hands were sliding up his thighs, the heated fingers probing at the taut muscles, rubbing in tight little circles along the hypersensitive flesh there, creating sensations that took his breath.

She smoothed her hands along his thighs as she mouthed his cock, suckling the head just past her lips. Her hot tongue rimmed beneath the crest, her fingers, slick from the sweet moisture she was spreading over his cock, glanced over his anus.

"Enough." He could barely push the words past his lips as he buried his hands in her hair, holding her lips where he needed them most. Those wicked little fingers were another story, though.

Her sharp teeth raked over the head of his cock, a warning, violent pulse of pleasure shooting to his testicles before she enclosed the straining crest once again. The erotic message was clear. She would do what she wanted, not as he willed.

"Jessie, baby..." His hands clenched tight as her little fingers probed, her tongue stroked. He was going to lose his mind any minute. If she did what he suspected she was about to.

"Fuck!" A fingertip penetrated the entrance as his hands clamped on her hair, driving his cock several inches into her sucking mouth before she could stop him. "Pay the price, little girl," he snarled, his hips shifting as her finger slipped in further. "You want to be bad, then you're going to get your face fucked in return."

The explicit words had her groaning, the vibration tingling along his erection as her fingertip slid back, gathered moisture and returned with a friend. Two slender tips slipped inside him. His hips jerked again, moving, thrusting his cock into her mouth as her tongue flickered hungrily around it.

She was hesitant, not really certain. Her dark eyes gazed up at him as she obviously fought to retain enough of her own control to be certain he was enjoying her efforts towards his pleasure.

"Anything you want, baby girl," he growled, holding her head in place, fighting to gather enough breath to speak. "Experiment. There's not much I wouldn't let you do..."

Her fingers slid in, glancing over a spot that sent pleasure thundering so hard, so viciously through him, his head fell back and a hoarse shout spilled from his lips. Damn, she was killing him with pleasure. Her mouth sank on his thrusting cock, his hips driving the thick length as deep into her mouth as she would allow him.

When her fingers returned, unerringly finding that spot that destroyed his control, she worked it for all she was worth. Thrusting easily, stroking over it, massaging it, manipulating it until his hands held her in place, his hips driving his erection to the back of her throat before his balls erupted. He felt his seed erupt from the tip of his cock, splashing into her rapidly swallowing throat before another brutal pulse ripped from him.

It seemed never-ending, locking his muscles painfully as he clamped down on her fingers and his cock spewed into her suckling mouth.

"Enough." He felt like an animal, wracked by lust so pervasive, so overwhelming there was no thought, nothing but instinct.

His hand moved to clamp onto her wrist, drawing her fingers from his ass before he pushed her back to the mattress. For what he had mind, nothing would do but a bed. A bed and the silky, slick slide of her desire on his lips, his tongue, feeding the fury of lust raging through him.

Jessie cried out as Slade tossed her to the bed, her hands reaching for him only to have him stretch them above her head.

"Stay!" The harsh growl was a warning, a command she obeyed instinctively as she watched him move to the small chest across from the bed. He jerked it open, retrieving the anal wand he had bought and stored there the day before, and the tube of lubrication lying beside it, before he pushed her thighs open and moved between them.

He didn't give her time to catch her breath. No time to prepare, no hesitant licks or gentle kisses to her thighs. He dove into her pussy, his tongue parting the bare curves, his lips moving over her clit and proceeding to make her insane.

Her cry shattered the room as she arched to him. Her thighs fell apart as he pushed at them, his hands moving between her thighs before she felt him lifting her hips higher, shoving a pillow beneath them.

She thrashed beneath him as his tongue whipped over her cunt, licking, stroking, circling her clit and teasing her past bearing as she felt the anal wand pressing against the entrance to her ass.

"On my shoulders," he growled, lifting her feet until they rested on his broad shoulders, leaving her completely open to him.

His mouth worked over her flesh with devastating results. He sucked at her clit, his tongue flickering until she tightened, so close to orgasm she could feel the ripples beginning in her womb.

He pulled back.

"No. Damn you..." she cried out raggedly, then her back arched, her hands gripping the wood rails of the hcadboard as she felt the anal wand sink past the first circular ball.

His tongue plunged inside her weeping pussy again, pumping erotically, erratically, sending her senses spinning as he licked at the tender walls. Her nerve endings clashed, blazed.

He pulled back.

"Slade..." she wailed his name, pleading.

The wand sank in several more degrees, stretching her further as the rounded balls it consisted of grew larger.

"Hot, sweet, little pussy," he crooned, licking through the slit, tonguing the fold as he blew several warm, heated pulses of air toward her clit. "There, sweet baby. You like this?"

Her feet pressed into his shoulders as she lifted, fighting to press closer. His tongue began to rim the entrance to her vagina, flickering over the opening, lapping at the juices falling from her.

He was teasing her to death.

The wand slipped in further, sending fire streaking through her anus as it began to stretch wider, to send a startling mix of pleasure/pain rocketing through her. Her pussy spasmed as she cried out, her voice rough, strangled even to her own ears.

"How pretty." He eased back, sinking the wand inside her one degree deeper as she jerked in his grip. "That sweet bare pussy is intoxicating, Jessie. All silky and slick." He licked at the folds again, causing her to jerk with the pleasure. "We're going to see how much of that wand you can take." His smile was dark, sensual. "Then I'm going to fuck you, Jessie. I'm going to sink inside your pussy, and it's going to be hotter, tighter, so fucking tight I'll have to work in slow and easy…"

She was going to come from his words alone. She shuddered, crying out as the wand eased in by another notch. She lowered her hands, reaching for him.

"Put the hands back!" His voice was sharp, controlled.

Jessie jerked back, her fists balling in the comforter beneath her rather than the hard muscles of his arms.

"Good girl," he crooned, his hand smoothing over the curve of her ass before he lifted it. A second later it descended again, arching her hips, sending fire racing through her ass.

She was lost in sensations that built, one upon the other, streaking through her nerve endings, blazing out of control as she fought the increasingly desperate need for orgasm. An orgasm he held just out of reach.

"Pretty baby," he whispered, leaning forward to suck her clit into his mouth, to tongue it gently as she twisted in his hold. "There you go, baby. Just let it all feel good."

She lost her breath as the wand sank in further, stretching her, burning her, as his head moved lower, his tongue plunging into her pussy. Her eyes widened, a gasp leaving her lips as she felt his tongue stretching her. The knobby extension in her rear was pressing into her pussy, making her tight, snug.

Slade chuckled, the sound one of dark hunger. "Oh yeah, sweetheart. I think we're ready now."

He crawled over her body, pausing at her breasts, his lips and tongue tormenting her hard nipples as the head of his cock brushed against her pussy. Breathing brokenly, her senses dazed, she moved against the heat and hardness pressing against her as the firm tugs of his mouth at her nipples sent agonizing pleasure streaking to her clit.

He stole her breath, moving from her breasts to her lips, his teeth tugging at the lower curve as he filled her vision.

"Ready, baby?" The flared, too-wide head of his cock pressed against the entrance to her cunt. The folds parted slowly before wrapping around the wide crest. He paused.

"Let me taste your kiss, Jessie. Give me your lips, baby," he whispered.

She moaned brokenly, her head tossing against the mattress, her hips writhing beneath his as she opened her lips.

She could taste herself, a strangely sweet taste that clung to his lips, to his tongue as he kissed her with such gentleness she could feel it sinking into her heart.

"I love you, Jessie," he whispered against her lips. "I love you more than life."

She screamed, bucking against him, her hands clamping to his shoulders as he began to work his cock inside her. Fire, a blazing conflagration of sensation, pleasure/pain, heat and hardness working slow and easy inside her, shifting the wand embedded in her ass even as he filled her pussy.

"Oh God. Slade... Slade... More." She was stretched on a rack of sensation, violent, intense, pushing her close, so close to orgasm her womb was rippling with it. So close but not yet.

He pushed inside her, retreated, thrusting deeper with each impalement until she was shaking, shuddering, so filled with him she was certain he had penetrated her soul.

"There, baby." He was in her to the hilt, throbbing, hot, blistering her with passion and need. Lust was like a whirlwind inside her, spinning through her dazed senses as she whimpered, cried. "Here we go, darlin'." He kissed her lips again, a slow benediction of feeling before his hips shifted and he began to move.

He began slow. Slow and easy, working inside her with each thrust as she strained closer to release. Within minutes he was moving faster, harder, testing the limits of her arousal, her pleasure, holding her on the edge, making her wait until her legs lifted further, wrapped his hips and she pleaded.

"Fuck me, Slade. Fuck me hard. And fast and deep...and... Oh. God."

She was gone. There was no longer just Jessie. Her screams filled her head, or were they his, as he began to pound inside her, shuttling in and out, jackhammer strokes that pierced her senses and rocketed her to the stars.

Her orgasm was violent. It tore through her. It burned her. It shook every bone and muscle in her body. It shattered her mind, swept through her with the force of a cataclysm before hurling her into space. Stars exploded in front of her eyes, swept through her mind. It left her drifting in a haze of harsh, violent aftershocks. The feel of Slade shuddering above her, the heated pulse of his seed blasting inside her, triggered a bone-wracking tremor, a startled whimper, and then left her to drift back to earth in peace.

"I live for you, baby. Always..." he whispered at her ear, his voice hoarse, throbbing with pleasure and emotion and all the dreams she had ever held.

Her eyes drifted open, staring back at him as his lifted just enough to watch her.

"I live for you," she whispered. "Always, Slade. Always and forever..."

Epilogue
One Year Later

Fireworks were exploding in the air, kids were running, jumping, screaming with all the exuberance of youth as laughter and revelry filled the riverbank clearing. In the middle of the throng of children, one little boy laughed mischievously, pulling at the pigtails of one of the older girls before scampering out of harm's way. He might have pulled it off if the shorts he wore weren't sliding down his rump.

But because they were, he paused, giving the teenager time to catch up with him, her fingers finding sensitive ribs and sending him into gales of laughter before the girl bussed him on the cheek with a big kiss and sent him on his way.

From beneath the awning of the RV, Jessie and Slade watched, laughing at Cody's antics as Slade's hands ran once again over Jessie's still flat stomach. On his wide finger a band of gold glittered in the firelight, the mate to the one she wore with the simple diamond on her finger. She hadn't wanted a larger diamond; Jessie wasn't one for flash, and as much as Slade had wanted to buy the more expensive, flashier stones, he had gone with what he had known Jessie would like best.

She had cried. When he had gone to his knee in front of her, slipping the ring on her finger and whispering how much he loved her, she had cried. Which amazed Slade. He would have thought by then she would have been pretty damned certain she was the center of his life. He couldn't keep his hands off her, keeping her naked as often as possible.

Not that she had given in to the idea of marriage easily. And she wouldn't move in with him until they were married because of Cody. She had wanted them to have time, to give Cody time to get used to her, to accept her, not just as his daddy's girlfriend or wife, but as his mother. With Glenna and Hank's disavowal of the child, she had taken him as her own, sheltering him, guarding him at school like a mother hen. Clarissa Jennings hadn't known what hit her the first time she had dared to speak sharply to the child while in the hallway, when Cody had followed the other children's urging and asked her if she was his cousin.

Jessie had left her room as the woman waspishly replied that Cody had no cousins. The story had sped through the county. How Jessie had smiled coldly, gripped the other woman's arm in a bruising grip, and hauled her off to her own office. The screaming match that ensued had been heard throughout the school. When Jessie left, she smiled politely to the wide-eyed parents in the office, told the secretary she and Cody would be leaving for the day for the superintendent's office and then her lawyer's office. After they collected Cody's father.

No one would ever hurt Cody again, she made sure of it. She would be just as protective with all their children, Slade knew.

Cody glowed within the family atmosphere, something he had never known before. His laughter came more quickly, his solemn silences less often. Jessie had even convinced him to try swimming, with a sturdy lifejacket in place.

Slade's fingers played over the softness of her belly, rubbing, stroking, loving the feel of life he imagined he could sense there. Their baby. Six months after their marriage and she was giving him one of the greatest gifts in the world. A family. Not just her love, her love and acceptance of Cody, her desire for more children, the nurturing, loving heart that filled their days with warmth.

"You're too quiet," she murmured, her hands laying over his as she leaned against him, her eagle eye following their son as he laughed and romped.

The adults on babysitting duty were in force, and amazingly adept at their job. Jessie took nothing for granted though. She watched their son, claiming it was the only way to be sure.

"Thinking about you." He nuzzled her ear, tugging at it gently with his teeth, feeling the shiver that raced over her.

"You can't kidnap me." She laughed. "Cody will fight you for me."

Slade grunted. If Jessie was possessive over that kid, then Cody was even more so over her. That was *his* mommy, he told anyone who listened. And they better be nice to his mommy or he would fight them. That included Slade. They couldn't argue, Jessie always won. Simply because Cody stood in front of her, frowning fiercely, informing his father that *his* mommy was always right and daddies were just supposed to know that. Then he would hitch his always too big jeans on his bony hips like a little man and stalk away.

And though he hated to admit it, she was usually right.

"That boy has to go to sleep eventually," he growled, feeling his cock come to full screaming life as he pressed against her ass.

She snuggled closer to him, her smile bright enough to rival the fireworks as they found Cody again, watching as he dragged his teacher across the clearing to the RV where Slade and Jessie had set up lounge chairs. Annie Mayes was an angel as far as Cody was concerned. She was a pretty little thing, Slade admitted, watching her shy smile as she came near them.

"Cody insisted." Her laughter was a little self-conscious.

"Mommy, can I have another hot dog?" Cody hitched his shorts, straightened his shoulders and stared up at Jessie with charming devilry. "I'm hungry."

"You're always hungry." She laughed. "They're on the table inside. Go ahead. But no soda, Cody. Milk."

"Shew. I like soda, Mommy," he protested with a fierce frown.

"Remind me to pay Jazz back for this," she muttered at Slade before turning her attention back to Cody. "No soda. Milk or water, no arguments." He opened his mouth to do just that.

"Son. Mommy said no argument." Slade hardened his voice, knowing Jessie's soft spot, her hesitancy in this early stage of parenthood to his stubborn son. "Milk or water. Period."

His lips set in a pout. "Fine. But when I get big, I'm gonna drink soda all the time, just 'cause I like it." He stomped into the cabin, sighing loudly, arguing to himself as he got his hot dog and one of the small cartons of milk Jessie kept for him in the cooler.

"Annie, welcome to the party." Jessie stepped forward as Slade's hand slid down her arm, catching her hand as they faced the quiet teacher. "I'm glad you came tonight."

"Thanks." She shifted, embarrassed or maybe uncomfortable. "I'm not really used to parties."

She was Jessie's age, in her second year of teaching, and though Jessie assured him Annie was a perfect teacher, she seemed uncertain around many of the parents. Especially the men. The first day of school, her room bombarded by Slade, Zack and Jazz, she had looked frankly terrified.

That look returned a second later when a hard thud from inside Jazz's RV caused her wide eyes to fly to the shadowed recesses of the RV parked beside theirs.

"Hey, Slade. Damn it, Zack stole my drinks again and just drove off with some city girl. That boy needs to buy his own damned liquor." Jazz bounded from his camper, his big body landing heavily, his expression glowering as he glanced at them before stepping into Slade and Jessie's RV. "Or did Jessie make you get rid of the good stuff... Oh hi, squirt. I got soda in my place, why are you drinking milk?"

Jessie sighed. Slade chuckled. Annie looked terrified.

"I have to go." Annie backed into the awning support as Jazz stepped out again. Dressed in cut-off shorts and nothing else, standing nearly six feet, six inches in bare feet with that wild mane of black hair falling to his shoulders and those icy Viking-blue eyes, he could be a forbidding sight.

"Hey, little mouse, where are you scurrying off to?" He laughed as she jumped back again before moving quickly along the bank. "Was it something I said?" He waggled his brows, turning to Slade with a white, sharp smile.

Slade shook his head, watching as Jazz made off with the last bottle of whisky, his laughter echoing behind him.

"You have strange friends." Jessie turned in his arms, peeking into the dimly lit RV to catch sight of Cody camped in front of the cartoons, hot dog in one hand, milk in the other. "I think he deliberately ran Annie off."

"Ah, but I have the best wife." He bent his head, kissing her neck, his hands running down her back as he rubbed his erection against her belly. He was not going to get into a discussion of Jazz's shortcomings. The list was just too damned long. "Wanna get kidnapped?"

She lifted her head, her smile bright, her eyes shining with love, passion and a heated warmth that still had the power to make his heart thunder in his chest.

"Anytime, stud," she whispered. "Anytime." She glanced in the cabin. "Well, after Cody goes to sleep maybe."

Their laughter mingled then became silent. In the glow of the bonfire, lit by the fireworks above, Slade's lips covered Jessie's, smoothing over them, sinking into a caress that stroked his soul.

His wife. His family. And life was good.

Lora Leigh

To learn more about Lora, please visit www.loraleigh.com. You can email to her at loraleigh02@aol.com, join her Yahoo! group to join in the fun with other readers as well as Lora http://groups.yahoo.com/group/loraleighchatters or keep up to date with Lora's events by joining her newsletter http://groups.yahoo.com/group/SensuousEscapes.

Blackmailed
(C) 2006 Annmarie McKenna

An erotic contemporary romance ménage available in digital formats May 30 at Samhain Publishing and coming soon in paperback...

Brianna Wyatt may be a victim of her father's machinations, but one look is all it takes for Cole Masters and Tyler Cannon to offer her their own style of ménage a trois blackmail.

Brianna Wyatt's father is blackmailing her into doing what he wants by threatening to send her brother to an institution. She would do anything to keep that from happening, including go along with his demented scheme of her getting pregnant by Cole Masters--a man who's been rumored to share a woman with his best friend, and who leaves Brianna's innocent senses in shambles.

Cole is sure he's about to be blackmailed—why else would a man whore his daughter? But there's something about her that neither Cole nor his best friend, Tyler Cannon, can deny. They want her, and don't hesitate for a second on making their own offer. Her brother's protection for her body.

When danger flirts with Brianna's life, there is nothing they won't do to keep her safe. Including listening to what their hearts are saying.

Warning: this title contains graphic language, hot, explicit sex, bondage, domination/submission and ménage a trois and is not for the faint of heart!

Enjoy this hot, steamy, sensual excerpt from Blackmailed...

"I know you're awake, Bri."

"Cole?" She turned her head, searching for the source, knowing it hadn't come from her left.

"Yes, sweetheart?"

There he was, at her feet. She swallowed. "Who's here, Cole?"

"You're right. She does swallow when she's nervous."

Two distinct laughs reverberated in her ears. She fought to see through the blackness, to see who she was dealing with, while her body thrilled and betrayed her. She felt the slick evidence of her desire pooling with the thought of being touched by two men, even when her mind screamed it was wrong to want to be fucked by more than one.

Apparently the rumors about Cole were true. She should feel embarrassed, outraged that they were both looking at her naked body, but she couldn't summon up either emotion.

The feather, at least she thought it was a feather, stroked her exposed neck like a lover's caress, soothing her despite her fears.

"Shh. Relax," the man whispered against her ear.

His fingers, she assumed they were the unknown man's, trailed a blazing path down her throat, along the valley between her breasts, pausing to circle her areolas. His fingernails scraped gently across her abdomen and stopped where he dipped into her belly button. Brianna sucked in a breath at the exquisite feelings. It was then she realized she was also bound to the bed by a strap across her hips, preventing her from even arching her back.

Her face grew red as she smelled her own arousal.

"So soft," he murmured.

"Like silk," Cole agreed.

The strange fingers continued their journey, learning her body and tangling in her pubic hair. Brianna bit her lip, silently begging him not to stop, to touch her clit, to make her come, but he withdrew his hand. She groaned in disappointment and sank into the mattress.

"Let's shave this off. I want only skin here."

Brianna gasped at the gruff command, startled by his abrupt change from gentle to demanding.

"A hot, wet towel, Bri." The bed dipped between her legs where she guessed Cole climbed closer to her.

"Cole, stop. I don't want this. Don't do this!" She sounded pathetic, she knew, but God, they had her tied to a bed and were going to shave her pussy.

"You promised, Bri. It was part of our bargain. You agreed to do anything I asked of you. Now I'm telling you. You will do whatever we tell you. Now, shh. We want you naked, Bri. We want to feel your smooth skin as we lap up your juices. It's just hair, baby."

"We? We?" Brianna squirmed as best she could. "Who is we? Damn it, Cole, at least let me see who we is!"

"My name is Tyler." He said this one second before an intense pain shot through her nipple. She screamed and tried to dislodge whatever was pinching her now distended, hard nipple. The tight bead was soothed as quickly as it had been punished by a wet tongue rasping over it. Immediately the pain became a pleasure sizzling its way to her vagina, drenching the hair which would soon be gone.

Suddenly she didn't care what they did to her pubic hair, she just wanted one of them to touch her.

"A screamer, huh?"

"I told you she was."

"You made it sound like she was a little noisy, not loud enough to shake the rafters."

"Yeah, well, I wanted you to see for yourself."

Brianna mentally pictured Cole's shrug and nearly cleared her throat as they talked about her as if she were not there. Her nipple was throbbing beneath its clip, a delicious, warm tingle, now that the pain had dissipated.

"Please," she begged, her body again doing the speaking for her.

"Please what?" Tyler asked.

There was no emotion in his words, as if he didn't care that he had a tied-up, naked woman laid out like a sacrifice in front of him.

"Please, touch me. Cole," she offered at the last second, remembering his desire for her to say his name.

"You remembered. I'm impressed."

He touched her then, laying the hot washrag over her mound. The heat scorched her raised clit, adding to the searing pleasure/pain at her nipple. Her body hummed with desire.

Warm lips closed around her free nipple, sucking it into a hard peak. Tyler, she thought, rolled it around his wet mouth, consuming her. She moaned and ground her head into the mattress. Cole laid his hand over her washrag-clad pussy and pressed in rhythm with the mouth sucking her breast. Its rough texture antagonized her clit, but did not give her enough.

She wanted to touch someone, to feel the hardness of Cole's body against hers as he devoured her. Even more perverse, she wanted to slide her hands over Tyler's skin, to learn the shape of him through touch, if she would not be allowed to look at him.

His lips released her tight bud with a pop one second before it was clipped the same as its twin. She screamed and bit into her lip, tasting the coppery fluid leaking onto her tongue.

"Oh, God. Oh, God." She thrashed her head back and forth, denying the shooting pulses of pain grinding away at her chest. Her nipples burned deliciously as a tongue once again soothed the offended flesh. One touch to her clit would send her over the edge, but now she realized the rag had been lifted and the hot wetness was gone. A cool breeze wafted through her pubic region, cooling her desire.

"Please!" she pleaded, unashamed now that she was so close.

"Not yet, little one."

Samhain Publishing, Ltd.

It's all about the story...

Action/Adventure
Fantasy
Historical
Horror
Mainstream
Mystery/Suspense
Non-Fiction
Paranormal
Red Hots!
Romance
Science Fiction
Western
Young Adult

http://www.samhainpublishing.com